C000091597

A STOLEN SEASON

A Regency Time Travel Romance

TAMARA GILL

COPYRIGHT

A Stolen Season
Copyright © 2014 by Tamara Gill
Cover Art by EDH Graphics

This book is a work of fiction. The names, characters, places, and incidents are products of the writer's imagination or have been used fictitiously and are not to be construed as real. Any resemblance to persons, living or dead, actual events, locales or organizations is entirely coincidental.

All rights reserved. Without limiting the rights under copyright reserved above, no part of this publication may be reproduced, stored in or introduced into a database and retrieval system or transmitted in any form or any means (electronic, mechanical, photocopying, recording or otherwise) without the prior written permission of both the owner of copyright and the above publishers.

ISBN-13: 9781973269564

DEDICATION

*For my beautiful mum, who's loved and believed in
A Stolen Season as much as I always have.*

CHAPTER 1

ENGLAND 1817 – Kent

Sarah shifted in the saddle, the weight of her saturated clothes heavy on her shoulders and hindering her seat. The horse's pounding hooves, as loud as a drum, echoed in her ears. She kicked her mount and urged him over a small hedgerow, her determination not to be caught overriding her common sense.

Rain streamed down her face, but she couldn't stop. The future of TimeArch depended on it. Her father's years of research. The hundreds of hours spent working on man's greatest, most sought-after ability. Sarah slowed her mount to canter through a fast moving ford, the stones causing the horse to stumble, making the short trip across painfully slow. Time was up. She had to get away. Though the horse grappled and slipped up the other side of the muddy bank to continue on, apprehension still threatened to close her throat in panic.

The mount missed a step, and Sarah clutched the saddle, cursing the weather. She flashed a glance over her shoulder and cried out her frustration into the sheeting rain at the sight of the Earl of Earnston not two horse-lengths behind.

His gaze held hers, and with fearless determination, he urged his mount beside, clutching for her reins.

"Let go." Sarah punched his hand and kicked out, trying to push him away. All in vain, as it seemed nothing could deter his resolve.

"What does it do?" he yelled, pulling on her reins.

The horses bumped hard, and Sarah fought for balance. "Let go, Lord Earnston. You'll kill us both."

He released her reins for a moment as a large bush separated them. But, at blistering speed, he drew beside her again.

"What's so important you'd risk your life?" he hollered over the storm.

Sarah shook her head. Why wouldn't he leave her alone? Damn her clumsiness in his library. Had she never knocked over the vase—had she not tripped, for that matter—the Earl would never have investigated the sound. But he had, and he'd found her hands deep in his collection of peculiars, stealing a device not of this time.

"Forget about it. Forget me," she yelled through the deluge. "Go home!"

"No," he said, spurring his horse ahead of hers.

A low-lying tree branch slapped her face. Sarah cringed at the stinging pain. The night was perfect for thievery, but not for escape at breakneck speed. If they kept up the chase, it was only a matter of time before one of them was killed.

"Stop your horse!"

Sarah shook her head and kicked her mount on. No matter the dangers, she couldn't obey him. The future, her father's business, everything she held dear hinged on her getting away. "I won't. My lord, please leave me."

He clasped her reins and jerked hard. Sarah's horse bucked at the aggressive manhandling, and she tipped awkwardly to one side. Feeling herself about to fall, she reached out and clutched at the earl. Her reins slipped from his grasp as his strong arm encircled her waist, struggling to keep her from falling between the two horses. But it was little use. Her horse veered away, and she fell hard against his lordship's mount. Her fingers, cold and wet, slipped for purchase on his saddle, but his horse shied away from her.

"Hold on, I have you." With an oath, the earl tried to pull her up, but gravity was against them.

"I'm slipping. Let me go. I'll bring you down." Sarah's feet dragged on the muddy, stone-strewn road, and she braced herself for a bruising fall. A gentleman to the last, he shook his head and tried to pull up his horse. "Please, let me go." But it was too late. His horse slipped, and they both hit the muddy track with a sickening thud.

Sarah landed on her knees and rolled. Leaf litter and mud entered her mouth, and her leg twisted, shooting a pain into her hip.

Moments later, the wet nose of her horse nuzzled her neck. She dragged herself to a sitting position and wiped mud from her face and eyes with a torn remnant of her shirt. Taking deep breaths, she waited for her body to stop shaking. The only sound was the rain slapping at the leaves through the foliage above.

Then she saw the motionless form on the muddy track. Dread clawed up her spine. Sarah crawled to where the earl lay, his head twisted at an awkward angle. She rolled him over and cursed his vacant, lifeless eyes.

"Don't be dead. Please, don't be dead." She felt along his stubbled jaw and around to the nape of his neck where a lump protruded from his skin.

Unable to accept what her eyes told her, she bent over his chest and listened for a heartbeat.

Nothing.

Sarah slumped back on her haunches and covered her face. She'd killed him. She'd killed Lord William, the blooming Earl of Earnston! "I'm so sorry," she said, tears mingling with the rain in a muddy pool at her feet. What had she done? The earl wasn't supposed to die, not yet, and certainly not by her hand. Within the space of half an hour, she'd probably wiped out a complete generation of earls. She'd stuffed up history, and she couldn't undo it.

Not even her father could.

A crack of lightning illuminated the dark forest, and Sarah quickly stood when the silhouette of a horse and man loomed from the shadows.

"Halt!"

Ignoring the warning, she grappled to mount her horse as the fired-up mare pranced. "I'm sorry," she said to the cloaked figure as he dismounted and ran to the earl's limp form sprawled on the ground.

He bent, felt for a pulse, and gasped. Her stomach rolled with nausea knowing what she'd done and what he'd discovered. A flicker of silver flashed as he stood.

"Stay where you are or I'll shoot you as dead as my brother."

Sarah turned her head, frantically searching for someone to help. Perhaps Richard, her partner, who'd warned her not to go tonight. He said the weather wasn't good for safe getaways.

And he was right.

It was the flash of lightning outside the earl's library window illuminating a menagerie of severed and stuffed animal heads that had scared the shit out of her, and she'd

tripped. The earl heard the commotion, came to investigate, and caught her red handed.

Idiot.

"Please. It was an accident." She watched him cock the
pistol and wondered if he'd actually shoot a woman. His
voice, trembling with shock and hate, told her he would.

"Get off the horse—now."

"I can't." With shaking fingers, she grabbed the reins.
"I'm sorry." She turned her horse and kicked it hard.

"Halt, I say."

She ignored the steely voice that thrummed with warning. Instead, she pushed her mount into a gallop, the horse
slipping, unable to move fast enough. And then the shot,
followed by searing pain, deafened her and deadened the
sound of the thrashing storm to a vague rumble.

Her fingers tingled and warmth seeped along her skin.
Sarah looked down, expecting to see her arm missing. He'd
shot her! "Get up," she hollered to the horse, ignoring the
pain and the curse from behind.

The horse gained its footing, and she peered over her
shoulder, the silhouette of the man all she could see. Cold
rain set goose bumps over her skin, yet she pushed on,
determined to make the inn and London. The second
decade of twenty-first century London to be exact.

WITH A RUNNING NOSE AND AN ARM THAT THROBBED AND
ached with every thud of the horse's stride, Sarah sped
through the night. At last, she spied the glowing lights of
the inn, a welcome beacon on this frightening journey.

Wet and bedraggled, like a beggar woman, she entered
the common room and waited for the innkeeper to
acknowledge her.

He walked toward her and eyed her injured arm with suspicion. "Ye have an injury there, lass. Do I need to summon the doctor for ye?"

"No. I'll be fine." She tried to pull what remained of her jacket across her wound, then gave up. She placed her sodden shawl about her shoulders, thankful she had thought to pack it in her saddlebag.

"What can I get ye then, love?" The innkeeper leaned on the counter, his fetid breath making her queasy stomach roll even more.

"Can you direct me to Mr. Alastair Lynch's room please? I believe he has a chamber set aside for a Miss Phoebe Marshall." A knowing twinkle entered his eyes, and Sarah's own narrowed in comprehension.

"Right this way, Miss Marshall."

The smell of wine, beer, and cooking meat permeated the air, making her nose twitch. She needed help and quickly. Summoning a smile, she thanked the innkeeper as he walked her to a door and nodded.

"This is ye're room, Miss. I'll send up a girl when I have one spare if ye wish for a wash."

"Ah, yes, thank you. That would be most kind." Sarah waited for his heavy footfalls to disappear down the stairs before she entered the chamber. The smell of damp wood burning and the flicker of two candles greeted her along with a pair of boots warming before the hearth.

Sarah shut the door and sagged against it. Relief poured through her veins, making her legs shake. The wound thumped, reminding her of the injury, and she pulled her shawl away to look.

Richard jumped from his seat. "Sarah, good God, you've been shot!"

"I have, but that's not the worst part. I also tripped in the Earl of Earnston's library and both brothers came to investigate. I ran." She walked over to the bed, threw her soggy shawl to the floor, and flopped onto the hard mattress. "He caught up with me when I escaped on horseback. How, I have no idea."

Richard came over and pulled her boots from her feet. "Knew the area, I suppose." He checked her wound. "It doesn't appear too bad. Just a graze by the looks of it."

Sarah glanced at the bloodied mess. "Yes. But that's not all. I killed Earnston."

Richard reeled as if slapped. "You killed the Earl… Good God! How? Why?"

She shook her head and gave him a rundown of the night's events. Sarah shut her eyes, not wanting to remember his lifeless gaze staring up at her or the horror of knowing she was the cause of his demise. "His brother came upon us and demanded I stay. Of course I ran. I had to. And…he shot me."

With one hand, she undid the first button at the front of her shirt, stood, and tried to pull the sleeve off her arm.

"Here, let me help you." Richard pulled out a knife. He cut the garment from around her arm and slid it down over the soaked chemise underneath.

Nausea pooled in her throat. "We have to go home. I need this wound seen to and…" "What?" he asked, brow furrowed.

"I don't feel well. It's not very nice being shot."

Richard chuckled, walked over to a bag in the corner of the room, and shuffled the contents. "I should imagine not. I think I have some morphine in here and a tetanus jab, also. Should be enough until we're home tomorrow."

Morphine sounded heavenly at the moment. A knock sounded at the door, and Richard allowed a wide-eyed maid to enter. With steady hands, she placed a steaming bowl of water and linens on a side table.

"Will ye be needing my assistance, Miss?" the servant asked, her eyes stealing to Richard, then back to her.

"No. Thank you. I shall be fine on my own." Sarah smiled and waited for the door to close before walking over to the water. She soaked a small cloth, dabbed it against the wound, and washed the blood from her arm. The injury was surprisingly clean—a flesh wound that wouldn't require stitching. A small mercy this night.

"Does it hurt?" Richard flicked the morphine needle. "Yes, so hurry up and give me the shot; you know I have a low pain threshold."

Within moments, the ache faded, and a warm fuzzy feeling settled over her. Richard fussed with her arm and bandaged it. Then she collapsed before the fire and stared at the flames that produced hardly any heat. What a mess she'd made of things. How was she ever to explain to her father?

"Are you good, then? I'll see you in the morning if so." Sarah nodded. "I'll be fine. The wound's hardly bleeding, and I intend to go to bed before the morphine wears off." She paused, knowing she had one more confession this eve. "Richard, I lost the mapping device."

He frowned. "You don't have it?"

"It was in my pocket, but it must have fallen out when I fell. I have no idea where it would be now."

He came and sat across from her, two fingers pinching the bridge of his nose. "Should we go back tomorrow and try and find it? Do you think the earl's brother knew what you'd stolen?"

"No," she said, standing and walking to the window to look out over the blackness illuminated at intervals by distant lightning. "Not yet at least. And with any luck the mud and rain has hidden the device, and all will be well.

Well, at least," she said, turning back to Richard, "until my father finds out what I did and the shit hits the fan."

"Shit's right." Richard paced the room, his footfalls loud in the small space. "This could be a disaster. Now he knows the device is valuable, for whatever reason, and will keep it hidden."

"That's if he finds it." She rubbed the bandage on her arm. "Let's not worry about it now. We'll be home tomorrow, and Father will tell us what to do."

"He certainly will. And let's hope for our sakes he's in a better mood than when he sent us here the first time."

Sarah sighed and pulled back the woolen blankets and coarse linen sheets on her bed. "Don't hold your breath. My father's going to be furious. Not only have I lost a device that could blow the lid off TimeArch and all its secrets, I've changed the history of a family forever."

☙❧

ERIC, NOW LORD EARNSTON, CURSED AND THREW HIS flintlock to the ground. Pain seized his chest when he glanced at his elder brother, dead at his feet. His eyes narrowed on the small female figure disappearing into the shadowy forest surrounding his family's estate.

He stumbled to his knees and allowed the rain to wash away tears shed for his closest confidant. A man of honor about to start a new chapter when he married his betrothed.

No longer. Thanks to the woman who'd snatched his future away.

He ran a hand through his hair, wondering why his brother had followed the chit at such breakneck speed.

With trembling fingers, he closed his brother's eyes, sending a prayer to God.

The woman had stolen something. But what?

He whistled for his horse, who, as if sensing death, hung his head lower with every step toward him. Eric lifted his brother, not an easy feat considering his size, and laid him over the saddle.

At the sound of crunching under his boot, Eric bent and frowned at the mud-soaked silver device beneath his feet. He rubbed it against his jacket and stared in amazement at the highly polished silver trinket.

A trinket his sibling had treasured for reasons Eric could never fathom.

With another rolling boom of thunder, he mounted his horse and turned for home to announce the death of his much-loved brother, bury him, and see justice served on the wench who took his life. Then he would find out why the object was so valuable—and why his brother and the woman would risk their lives to possess it.

CHAPTER 2

Present day. England – Reading

Sarah struggled to extricate herself from the restrictive nineteenth century costume, kicked it across the room, and plunged onto her bed. Their split-second journey through nearly two hundred years of time had left her exhausted and weak. Not to mention her injured arm ached like a son-of- a-bitch.

Sarah caught a glimpse of her reflection in the mirror across the room and cringed. She looked like she'd been punched in the nose, and dark lines shadowed bloodshot eyes that drooped with tiredness. Her ebony hair hung lifeless about her shoulders and appeared in need of a good wash.

The shrill jangling of the phone startled her. She fumbled for her mobile, recognizing her father's number with a sense of dread.

"I want you at the TimeArch office in forty-five minutes." "Dad, I'm exhausted. Couldn't it wait 'til tomorrow?"

She already knew what his answer would be.

"The future of our organization is at stake, Sarah. The boardroom. Forty-five minutes." Her mouth was open to respond, but the other end of the line was dead. He meant it this time—she'd really blown it.

It took all of five minutes to throw on jeans and a white shirt, drag a comb through her hair, and shove her feet into a pair of shoes kicked haphazardly to the side of the front door. Within ten minutes, she was pulling into mid-morning traffic, headed for TimeArch.

⚜

Six pairs of accusing eyes regarded her across the boardroom table. Her father's were dark with disappointment.

"Again, apologies, Father. I had the device and lost it when I fell off the horse. I don't know what else to say."

"Yes, and now it could turn up anywhere and at any time with a multitude of questions as to how a modern device could be found in the nineteenth century." Harrison Baxter gestured with his hands. "I trusted you and Richard to get the mapping device back, quickly and efficiently. And what do you do?" He sat down and took a sip of his water. "You both botched the job."

"Don't involve Richard in this. It's entirely my fault. Richard advised me not to attempt the theft. I went anyway."

"Sarah," her colleague warned.

"Oh, don't worry, I blame you exclusively. Richard I blame for not having the balls to demand that you stay."

Guilt assailed Sarah at the verbal set down to her friend and fellow archaeologist. "Well, I've stuffed up and it's done now, so tell me what I can do to fix the problem.

The last thing we need is the device turning up in the London Museum…"

"What's next indeed?" Her father frowned and steepled his fingers beneath his chin. A tall, robust man, he often made the most confident of men quiver in their boots. Today it was Richard's and her turn.

"You'll need to go back, procure the device, and return home. The earl's family will be in mourning for twelve months. We're assuming the new earl has the device, so we'll calculate your return for the end of the mourning period. Best not to throw you in his path too soon, considering the circumstances. We don't want him recognizing you and having you charged for your atrocious mistake."

"I didn't mean for Lord William to die. And I don't appreciate you talking as if I did. I made an error that I'll have to live with for the rest of my life. You could at least show me some support." Sarah blinked back tears. The show of emotion was not appropriate in a boardroom.

"TimeArch and all its secrets could be exposed, Sarah. Such errors cannot be tolerated nor ignored just because you're the boss's daughter. You will both return and reside in London as brother and sister. We will make up a family name and title for you to use, and I will give you the famous London Season to procure the device by any means available. But be sure to stick to the plan and return home as soon as possible. You know the rules of time travel. For every year in the past, a week passes in the future. Do not fail me again." Her father met both Richard's and her eyes. "Either of you."

Sarah followed his departure and threw a pen across the table. "Why didn't I listen to you? It's all such a mess." She slumped back in her chair.

"Yes, but one we'll fix. Don't worry, we'll get the device back." He patted her shoulder. "Now, I suggest you end your pity party and prepare yourself for nineteenth century London and all its trappings. The 1818 Season awaits us."

Sarah groaned. *Why not?* Her life couldn't possibly get any worse....

London 1818 – Mayfair

"Well, this should be interesting." Sarah glanced around the grandly proportioned room and tried to act the part of a somber debutante well past her prime at twenty-four years of age.

"Stop glaring at everyone and remember to smile. Like this..." Richard offered her a blatantly fake grin.

She frowned. "We shouldn't be here. We weren't invited. I feel like everyone is looking at us."

Richard chuckled as he moved them into the throng. "They are."

After another jab at her side, Sarah plastered on the brightest smile she could muster. How ridiculous it was for her to even be here. She wasn't trained for balls and parties. She'd be much more relaxed digging for ancient artifacts in a pit than in Mayfair's ballrooms.

"This had better be the right house. I don't want to be dressed up like an innocent debutante for nothing."

Richard paused, searching the room before walking on. "We're in the Earl of Earnston's home, and this is the yearly ball he holds to keep his mother satisfied. And from the reports your father received, he is the gentleman who harbors our electronic mapping device. And there he is."

Sarah glanced over her shoulder to where he indicated and stilled. It was like witnessing Lord William's ghost. She'd never again thought to see eyes so dark a blue—especially not surveying the room with such a relaxed, studied air. The hairs on the back of her neck rose as she expected him to point a finger at her and shout *murderer* for all to hear.

She took a calming breath and refused to give in to her ridiculous fear. Instead, she turned to fully absorb his every detail. Like his brother, the new Earl was tall, athletic and oozed Old World charm. His dark brown hair was longer than that of the other gentlemen present, and even from this distance Sarah could see he wasn't a man to underestimate. "I forgot they were twins," she said.

"Are they similar?" Richard asked, tugging her arm so she faced him.

"Very." *Except this man was alive, virile, and altogether too handsome for his own good.*

Richard cleared his throat. "You're supposed to be a debutante, not a matron of the ton looking for her next dalliance. Perhaps you ought not to be so 'pointed' in your appreciation of the Earl—I'm worried he may go up in smoke."

Sarah scoffed and turned back. "I just hadn't expected him to be so…" *delicious*. "His appearance was so different the last time I saw him."

"You don't think he'll recognize you from that night, do you? He did see you in the library with his brother before he shot you out on the road."

"I don't think so. I only saw him for a split second at both locations. I think we'll be okay." She placed her arm through her supposed brother's arm. "So, how am I to do this? You cannot introduce me because you're not one of his acquaintances. His lordship must request such social introductions. And we know no one here to undertake the deed." Richard nodded, portraying an air of nonchalance she knew went only skin-deep.

"Do you think you could catch his eye, and perhaps

then he'll request an introduction?" He handed her a glass of champagne. Sarah took a sip and visually retraced her path to Lord Earnston. He had disappeared.

"Where's he gone? I can't see him."

"He's near the terrace doors, speaking to the dark beauty in the white gown." Richard's voice deepened in appreciation.

"I'm the one here to get close to the Earl. The only thing I want you getting close to is the mapping device, so keep your eyes off the waltzing fillies." Sarah shook her head. This was a waste of time. Her expertise would be better spent back at her dig site in southern Italy. And yet, here she was at a nineteenth century London ball about to seduce a strange man, and all because they'd been sloppy with their work.

Not that it would be a hardship to seduce *this man*, but still it irked that her father would request she undertake such a dirty deed. If she had it to do over, she would have bided her time in securing the mapping device as Richard had urged her.

She sighed.

"He's taking stock of the guests, Sarah. Start looking delectable."

"Delectable? I think you've been living in this society far too long. You're starting to sound like them."

Richard smiled and turned his gaze to the throng. Sarah checked her gown and pulled her shoulders back to accentuate her figure. Her hair was coiled atop her head with a string of diamonds threaded through her dark locks. She wore no other jewelry, but she knew her emerald gown would accentuate the color of her eyes. Gentlemen walking past smiled and nodded, their appreciative gazes almost salacious.

Sarah's attention settled on her quarry, who regarded

her with a quizzical brow from the back of the room. The lady hanging off his arm was chatting animatedly up at him. She was very pretty, probably his secret *chère-amie.*

Her eyes narrowed at the thought. The last thing she needed was competition for the gentleman's attention. She noted that although his suit was cut to perfection, he still had an air of ruggedness about him. Her interest strayed from his broad shoulders to his facial features. His mouth was sensual, his nose perfectly straight, but his eyes were dark and hooded and, right at this moment, locked on her.

She swallowed but didn't break the connection. Couldn't, if she was truthful. No wonder women of the era fooled around when an opportunity like him knocked on their doors. Allowing her lips to spread in a shy smile, she tried to hide her mortification when his lordship's brow furrowed with what appeared to be confusion and shock.

She tightened her grip on Richard's arm. "I think I just made a faux-pas."

Richard nodded to a passing couple, then turned his gaze on her. "Do I want to know what that is?"

Out of the corner of her eye, Sarah noted the earl cutting across the room toward them. "Let's just say, I think I have his lordship's attention. But perhaps not in a good way."

Not until his lordship came to stand before them did Sarah acknowledge his presence. He hadn't seemed as tall or as broad from a distance as he did hovering before her. Her belly knotted, either from the nerves that assailed her or the desire he aroused within her. She supposed the answer depended on what came out of his mouth in the next moment.

"Pray, do I know you?" the earl asked. It wasn't desire.

Richard bowed. "I am Lord Richard Baxter, Baron Stanley, recently from Rome. This"—Richard motioned toward her—"is my sister, Miss Sarah Baxter. We are new to town, arriving only yesterday in fact."

"From Rome, you say?"

The earl took in their clothing. "I don't recall your names on the invitation list. You understand this is a private ball."

Richard blanched and laughed, the sound awkward even to Sarah's ears. "I apologize, my lord, we did not know. We'll leave immediately if you wish." At the earl's nod of agreement Richard pulled her toward the closest exit.

"Well, that went well," Sarah said, trying to ignore the pointed stares of the haute ton.

Richard led her into a corridor, the entrance foyer just visible beyond the well-lit passage. "It did," he replied, his steps sure.

"I was being sarcastic," Sarah said, as she waited for her cloak.

"I know, but you're wrong. The Earl has seen you and duly taken note. He may have been indignant and annoyed by our uninvited presence at his ball, but I believe he was quite the opposite when he took you in." He accepted their coats and thanked the footman.

"And will ensure I don't grace any further balls this Season, thus ending our search for the mapping device. How am I supposed to gain access to his homes, his friends' homes, if he hates me? We should have made out I was your wife, looking to cuckold her husband."

"Sarah, debutante or wife, you never intended to sleep with the guy." He paused and met her gaze. "Did you?"

Their carriage pulled up, the horses stomping their feet in eagerness to be gone. Sarah climbed up and flopped onto the seat. "Of course not. But he doesn't know that. It would have made my life a lot easier had he not thought me a pure little debutante in her first season."

"Well, either way, he knows of us, and his interest was piqued. And being told to leave a major ball of the season could work in our favor." He tapped the hood of the carriage and it started to rumble down the drive, the gravel loud under the wooden wheels.

"That's where you're wrong." Sarah pulled off her gloves in agitation.

"I imagine everyone will be talking of us and wishing to know who we are and why we were told to leave. Trust me when I say, come tomorrow, many a calling card and invitation will arrive at our door. And we'll accept every outing until Lord Earnston is groveling at your feet and willing to bestow any gift for the honor of your presence."

"The gift of a mapping device?" Sarah flexed fingers no longer constricted in silk. The strictures of nineteenth century fashion could go to hell.

"Precisely. And then, my dear little sister, we can go home."

"You have it all worked out, dear brother. But you forget, the ton and their fickle ways will want nothing to do with us now that we've been slighted by a member of their set. For all your time traveling, I'm surprised I know something about this era that you do not."

"You exaggerate. We will not be ostracized because we failed to be invited to a ball. People, for all their wealth, would not slight us for such a pathetic reason."

Sarah shook her head. "They will, trust me on this. We may as well have given ourselves a case of the pox tonight. Nothing can help us now other than our wiles and ability to steal in the dead of night."

"I don't agree." A determined glint entered Richard's

eyes. "And we'll not be doing any stealing, either. Look at how that turned out last time."

Sarah beat back the cold shiver that ran down her spine.

She needed no reminder.

ERIC REGARDED HIS UNINVITED VISITORS AS THEY STROLLED through the multitude of guests and left his London establishment. He frowned, wondering how they'd gained entry since the footmen were supposed to check the invitations upon arrival.

He would have to have a word with his staff.

"She's a handsome one. Why did you send her packing?"

Eric turned to Lord Mettleston, a boyhood friend and his closest confidante since his brother's passing. "They were not invited. Frankly, I have no idea who they are."

Mettleston chuckled and passed him a drink. "Rumor has it they've taken up residence in the old McKenzie place. You should know the property as it's the only one to rival your own in size."

Eric ignored his friend's smirk. It didn't surprise him Mettleston knew of the couple and where they lived. He always knew the ins and outs of everyone's business—what surprised Eric was that he did not. Since his brother's early demise, London had become a frequent haunt, and not a lot slipped past him—or his mother's gossiping tongue. To miss two new members of their set—supposedly—was quite unusual.

"Pray tell me where you received such news?"

Mettleston tapped his nose. "Ah, a gentleman never tells, my good man."

"Lord Stanley, his name was," Eric said, ignoring the goading. "A Baron from Rome." Eric nodded to a passing acquaintance and sipped his whisky, a fine vintage from his Scottish estate. "Who ever heard of a Baron from Rome? Or for that matter, such a name?"

"Well, it seems they're here to stay and looking for a foothold in society." Mettleston paused. "Had you really not invited them? Perhaps your mother did without your knowing."

"No, the final list passed my desk less than a fortnight ago. Their names were not on it." Eric smiled as his favorite cousin Lady Anita strolled toward them. Dressed in a stunning silk gown of light blue, many an eye turned her way, the majority of them not female.

"Eric," she said, clasping his arm before tapping it with her fan. "I heard you sent a guest home. Is this true? Has my cousin lost all good manners on this wonderful eve?"

Eric inwardly groaned and glared at Mettleston's chuckle. "Indeed I did. They were not invited, and I find their audacity highly disrespectful and vulgar."

His cousin made an indelicate sound. "Oh, come, you are too proud. I feel sorry for them being made to scuttle off like naughty schoolchildren. When I meet this mystery woman in the park tomorrow, I shall take her under my wing and prove you wrong about them. I'm sure they're lovely, just not used to what's 'done' in London society. You know they've been hidden away in Rome, so it's no small wonder their manners are a little lacking."

"I forbid you to show a lack of manners to match those of that homebound couple, Anita." Eric raised his brows at his cousin. "The Duke of Winters's daughter should know better than to go galloping about Hyde Park introducing herself to strangers. Strangers who are not worthy of our acquaintance or trust. No one will invite them anywhere after their atrocious behavior tonight."

"I shall, and nothing you say will deter me. The lady seemed pleasant enough, and I'm sure I'll be safe with Mama in the family carriage."

Knowing he was defeated, Eric sipped his whisky. When Anita was determined, there were few who could change her mind. Stubborn as one of his thoroughbreds.

"I believe there is a set after this waltz, Lady Anita. Tell me your card is not full and allow me the pleasure of the next two dances," his friend chimed in.

Anita moved away from Eric's side and curtsied before Lord Mettleston. "I would be honored, Lord Mettleston. You'll find me with Mama beside the supper room doors."

Eric's lips twitched. The Duchess of Winters loved her food and seemed determined this night to make the supper room before anyone else. Not that he could blame her; the spread he had ordered for the ball was second to none.

Lord Mettleston sighed as Anita walked away, and Eric threw him a pitying glance. "Give over, my friend. You know Anita has Lord Kentum in her sights, and she's in his. Would be a foolish notion to chase a woman destined for another."

"True," Mettleston said, still staring in Lady Anita's direction. "But I can't help but think I would suit much more agreeably than Kentum. For starters I'm a trusted family friend, practically family already."

"Precisely." Eric chuckled. "Which is the one reason she would never marry you. As much as Anita loves her family, she does not want to marry someone so closely connected to it. Kentum suits her. Leave her be."

Mettleston pulled him toward the card room. "Any news from the Bow Street Runner? Any leads on William's death?"

"No." Eric reined in the anger and frustration the question triggered. A year had passed and nothing. Not one lead. It was impossible to comprehend. People did not just disappear from the face of the Earth. The would-be thief had to go somewhere. But where?

"What was the latest report?" Mettleston stopped and handed him another glass of whisky before moving away from the other guests to ensure privacy.

"From what we know, the woman I fired upon arrived a short time later at Westerham Inn under the guise of Miss Phoebe Marshall. She met a man there; the innkeeper was unable to produce a name for him, but he remembered the girl. Miss Marshall, a beauty, wet and muddy from the storm and trying to hide her injury with little success. A maid informed us Miss Marshall met a Mr. Alastair Lynch upstairs, alone, before receiving clean water and something to eat. They left the next day, presumably for London. From there, we've lost track of them."

"Lovers, one would assume, after something from your estate valuable enough for Will to hightail it after her on such a night to get it back."

"Yes," Eric said absently, stroking the device he carried with him every day in his coat pocket. A strange, silver metal casing that he'd not been able to open. "Something she will eventually come back to procure, and when she does, I'll be ready. I will not rest until I witness her hanging for the crime against my family and Will's betrothed."

Mettleston clapped him on the shoulder. "I am sorry for William's death, you know, and I hope you have your justice."

"Thank you." Eric noted Anita looking about for Mettleston now that the waltz was over. "I think your dance partner awaits, my lord."

Mettleston placed his crystal glass on a nearby table and smiled. "That she does. I bid you adieu."

Eric laughed as his friend walked into the throng. He watched them dance for a time, allowing the short break of solitude to cool his temper. It always spiked when talking of his brother and the Bow Street Runners' inability to track the culprits down. But he could bide his time, and wait for them to strike again.

This time, there'd be no escape. No disappearing into the night like a phantom on horseback. That woman would pay. He would ensure she did.

CHAPTER 3

HYDE PARK WAS a hive of activity on this summer's afternoon. Sarah allowed the warmth to penetrate her skin as she studied London's society, milling around them.

The carriages were so highly polished her reflection was visible in their paintwork. Some vehicles bore family emblems or coat of arms that signified the upper echelons of society, those who languished within their open equipages peered down with an air of aloofness on the walking populace.

Groups of friends congregated upon the lawns and under leafed trees, shading themselves while no doubt discussing matters of great importance. Namely, what they would wear to tonight's ball.

She took in the array of fashion on show. Some women chose to dress as she did in a simple afternoon walking gown with a bonnet. Other women chose to ride, their smart green and blue riding suits, profusely decorated with braids and frogging, accentuating their lithe forms. Their tall hats were decorated with feathers and plumes.

What a difference two hundred years made. Sarah's

afternoon gown, although comfortable, was nothing like the clothes she usually wore when walking through Hyde Park. Joe's Icon Jeans and a comfortable baby doll top was her normal style. She adjusted her bodice, wondering when she'd get used to the sense of nakedness the light, flowing material made her feel.

"You look fine." Richard pulled her along, walking them beside the gravel path known as Ladies' Mile, where the lawn underfoot was spongy and soft.

"Thank you, though it doesn't seem to matter. Last night really does seem to have stuffed up our only means into this society." Sarah smiled at a passing couple, but neither one ventured to speak. She sighed, wondering if they were being given the cut direct on purpose or due to a lack of introduction.

"I don't understand it. I was sure causing a scandal would ensure some invitations in this morning's post." Richard frowned.

"I told you so." She wrapped her hand around his arm. "How on earth are we to repair the damage or, more importantly, secure invitations to any parties in the coming weeks?" She pulled her velvet and straw bonnet forward a little to block the sun's rays. Lord Earnston's slight could mean many things for them while in London. The most concerning, of course, was that she and Richard would have to break into his lordship's home to find the mapping device. And that she hoped to avoid at all costs.

"I haven't figured that out yet, but give me time. Perhaps I can befriend him and gain us access to his home," he said optimistically.

Sarah nodded. "A game of cards perhaps at one of his clubs. Don't men of this era enjoy such pastimes? Perhaps try Whites or ask around."

"I can't just walk into Whites and sit myself down. You

have to be a member, or invited in by one. I'd be thrown out faster than I could order a whisky." He paused, and she felt the muscles in his arm tense. "Look pleasant, Sarah, it seems the first person wishing to make our acquaintance is heading straight for us."

Sarah turned to follow his line of vision. The woman was dressed in a green velvet riding gown. Her ebony hair matched the dark lashes about her eyes. A town beauty, very exotic looking for an English woman, and one, by her quickened pace and determined jaw, set on meeting them.

"Good afternoon, I'm Lady Anita Drake, and you must be Lord Stanley and Miss Baxter?"

Sarah curtsied as Richard, oddly quiet, tipped his hat. "Good afternoon, Lady Anita. It's a pleasure to meet you."

Lady Anita smiled. "No, it's my pleasure. I would have called upon you earlier today, but Mama had a previous engagement." She caught Richard's eye. "Would you mind your sister taking a short stroll with me? I have my maid; we'll be well chaperoned."

Sarah saw relief flicker and fade in Richard's eyes.

"Of course. I'll walk toward the Serpentine and meet you near that copse of trees if you like."

"Wonderful." Lady Anita took Sarah's arm and turned her toward the throng. "Let me start, Miss Baxter, by apologizing for my untoward behavior. I know it is not done to introduce oneself to strangers, especially without a prior introduction by a male member of my family. But it is only me, my maid, and Mama here today. I find, in certain situations, one must overlook the niceties and manners and do what we can with what we have available."

Sarah, relaxed by Lady Anita's candor, found herself laughing. The woman, for all her obvious wealth and youth, seemed quite modern in her ideas and speech. Both traits sat easy with her. "I totally agree."

"Excellent." Lady Anita waved to a passing carriage then returned her attention to her companion. "Now, no more of this Lady Anita. Anita will do just fine when we're in private, and I hope you'll allow me to call you 'Sarah'?"

"Of course." Sarah wouldn't dare disagree with anything at this point. They walked along the grassy verge, eventually coming upon a section of the park that was a little less crowded.

"You may not know this, Sarah, but I'm Lord Earnston's cousin. I heard how he treated you last eve, and felt terrible. I told him I'd find you and confirm you did not warrant such treatment."

"Thank you." Sarah's heartbeat quickened at the mention of the earl.

"He's new to the earldom, only taking up the reins twelve months past after the death of his brother. A terrible tragedy for the family. The brothers were very close."

"How awful." Sarah inwardly squirmed at the reminder. Still, the only reason her father had not killed her after she'd confessed her blunder was because the late Earl of Earnston had been fated to die from a riding accident a year after her disastrous mistake.

She had therefore not changed history. His lordship, although married by that time, had not produced any heirs. The relief was only short lived as her actions had still brought on his death earlier than it was meant to be. It was not something someone forgot—or ever forgave.

"It was a terrible injustice. William, that was his name, was a wonderful man. It is very sad to lose a family member so young. And Eric—I mean, Lord Earnston—is wary of everyone these days, and I apologize to you for his behavior. When I introduce you, I'm sure he'll redeem himself."

If Lord Earnston finds out what I've done, I'll be lucky not to end up hanging at the end of a rope.

"It was our fault entirely. We were not invited to his lordship's ball and shouldn't have presumed all would be well," Sarah said.

"Do not tax yourself. Lord Earnston will not hold your first steps into London society against you. And with my friendship, you'll soon be receiving many an invitation to the Season's best balls and parties." Anita pointed to a woman sitting in a barouche avidly discussing something with a couple standing beside her door. Sarah took in her highly polished equipage, the magnificent horseflesh, and wondered who the powerful matron was.

"That is Lady Cottlestone, my dear. She has been married twice. Once to a baron and now to a viscount. Wonderful woman, and one I want you to meet."

Sarah allowed Anita to walk them toward the woman whose wealth and power oozed from the carriage. Lady Cottlestone was a large woman, well fed by the looks of her waistline and floppy jowls. While Anita made the introductions, Sarah remained silent and wondered what the matron made of her. The woman's bland, non-expressive face left a lot to one's imagination.

"Welcome to London, Miss Baxter," Lady Cottlestone said, her gaze roaming over Sarah's person.

"Thank you, my lady." Sarah curtsied and waited for her to speak again. It was odd being nervous, especially since, in the twenty-first century, she was a career woman not usually fazed by meeting people. But this woman had an air of Quality and Old World candor that left her uneasy and unsure of herself.

"And what brings you to our fine city, Miss Baxter? The Season? Looking for a husband, perhaps?"

Sarah smiled. "My brother and I decided to return to

England after the death of our parents abroad. My brother, should he be here, would say I am actively looking for a husband. Whereas I would dispute this fact and tell you I'm here to enjoy my first London Season, and that is all."

Lady Cottlestone settled into her squabs, a pained expression on her visage. "I am sorry to hear about your parents, my dear. It is very sad when one's parents pass at a young age and leave a woman such as yourself to rely on a male sibling for marriage guidance. Where abroad were you from, Miss Baxter?"

"Rome, my lady." Sarah shifted her feet, then, conscious of her habit of fidgeting when trying to avoid difficult questions, stilled.

"Oh, how I love Rome. Such a wondrous city and wonderful people. If not a little too warm in the summer months. What were your parents' names, Miss Baxter? Perhaps I knew them."

"Our family name is Baxter. My father's title was Baron Stanley. My parents tended to shy away from society and its trappings." Sarah took a fortifying breath and hoped she would not forget the multitude of lies she was spinning. The last thing they needed was to be caught out before the mapping device was back in their hands. She would have to bring Richard up to speed on these false-hoods, too.

Lady Cottlestone frowned. "No, I do not believe I have met your dearly departed parents."

"I am so looking forward to your ball tonight, Lady Cottlestone. Do say you'll allow your guests the pleasure of the waltz this eve. I do so love the dance," Anita said.

"After seeing it permitted at Lord Earnston's last night, I have decided it should not offend those with a more deli-cate personality." Lady Cottlestone turned her attention back to Sarah. "As you heard, Miss Baxter, I am hosting a ball at my home, Hendon House, this evening. Do say you will attend with your brother. I will send around an invitation to you directly."

"Thank you, my lady. As I am not aware of other plans for this evening, we'll be honored to attend." Sarah sighed her relief. Their foothold in the ton was secure.

The two women stepped back as the highly sprung barouche pulled away, and continued down the grassy bank toward the Serpentine. Richard stood under some trees, his clothing and relaxed stance making him look like a true nineteenth century gentleman enjoying the air in the park.

"Your brother is not married, Sarah?"

"No. And from what I can tell, he is in no rush to become so." She smiled, but out of loyalty to her friend refused to laugh. Poor Richard—should he find out they were discussing him in such a way, would turn as red as a beetroot.

"Such a shame for he's very handsome. Maybe a nice English woman will steal his heart."

"Perhaps," Sarah said, as they came before Richard. "Thank you, Lady Anita, for your company. I've enjoyed our walk."

"It was entirely my pleasure, Miss Baxter. I look forward to seeing you tonight."

Sarah smiled at Richard, as Anita, accompanied by her maid, strolled toward her mother's carriage. The Duchess studied them, her features full of enquiry as to whom her daughter had been engaged with.

"Lady Anita has secured us an invitation to Lady Cottlestone's ball this evening," Sarah blurted as soon as they were alone. "She introduced me, and her ladyship invited us both. I'm sure tomorrow your silver salver at the front door will be full of invites. Hopefully some of them will be close friends of our earl."

Richard took her arm and started to walk from the Serpentine back toward Park Lane. "Is Lady Cottlestone a friend of Lord Earnston?"

"I think so. She was at his ball last night apparently, so they are acquainted. Why?"

"Perhaps we should make Lady Cottlestone's home the first house we search. I don't know if she collects peculiars like the late earl did, but we should at least eliminate her from our list while we have the chance."

"You think the current earl may have sold his brother's collection to one of his friends?" Sarah hadn't even thought of that possibility. It was feasible and yet, remembering the devastation she had seen on the earl's face when he realized his brother lay dead at his feet, something told her he would treasure such a collection instead.

"I do." They reached Park Lane where Richard hailed a hackney and helped her inside.

"Okay, we will search her ladyship's home, but I doubt we'll find anything there." Sarah turned to the window to soak up the bustle of nineteenth century London life. "I think Lord Earnston will still have the device. His brother had many peculiars around his library and obviously loved collecting them. I doubt Lord Earnston would sell it off. It's not like he's in need of finances."

Richard leaned against the seat and pulled off his hat. "True, but it won't hurt to inspect all the same. It would be a wasted opportunity if we never checked."

"Lady Anita offered to introduce me to his lordship tonight. I admit I'm a little nervous about the whole thing."

"Don't be. If you start acting offish and tense, he may suspect or mistrust you, Sarah."

"I know. But I feel so guilty every time I look at the man. How will I get through the next few weeks?"

"His brother's death was an accident. He tried to save you. That he fell awkwardly was not your fault. The late Lord Earnston wouldn't blame you."

Sarah met Richard's gaze before looking away. She wasn't so sure the deceased earl wouldn't blame her. Yes, he might have been trying to save her from falling, but she'd stolen from his collection and engendered the reckless chase. "I just want to get the mapping device and go home. I've already done so much damage to this family. Let's work fast and get out of here." Normally a woman who bungled her way through life being too candid and dull, it required a Herculean effort for her to pull off playing a society queen.

Richard sat forward to open the door as the carriage pulled up before their rented Mayfair home. Built in the classical Georgian design, it seemed well pleased with its situation in life. Sarah followed Richard onto the sidewalk and started toward the front steps; a hired footman opened the front door before they had the opportunity to reach for the knob.

They walked into the library that overlooked Berkeley Square. Sarah laid her pelisse over a chair and tumbled into the chaise before the unlit hearth.

"We will work as fast as we can." Richard sat behind his desk and started to unfold the morning's paper. "You'll see. We'll be home before you know it, our errors remedied, and our continued employment with TimeArch ensured."

"I hope you're right," Sarah said, the awful dread still gnawing on her unease.

CHAPTER 4

THE HENDON HOUSE ballroom took Sarah's breath away. Guests mingled before them, their heels clicking against the parquetry floor, the women's gowns as bright as the jewels about their necks. Above them, grand chandeliers glistened with a multitude of wax candles, casting a golden hue on the scene.

It was amazing.

The Earl of Earnston's ballroom had been shrouded in a cloud of smoke by the time they had arrived the previous evening. Tonight, the gamblers hadn't yet graced the ballroom with their cigars.

"Welcome to Hendon House, Lord Stanley, Miss Baxter," Lady Cottlestone greeted them.

Sarah curtsied. "Thank you again for inviting us, Lady Cottlestone. We're so excited to be here tonight."

Her ladyship smiled and nodded. "My pleasure, my dear. Come"—she gestured toward the guests—"enjoy the ball. I believe you'll find Lady Anita near the supper room doors with the Duchess of Winters."

Sarah thanked her ladyship and took Richard's arm.

Social approval made their journey from one side of the room to the other quite the opposite experience of Lord Earnston's ball. Tonight, although no one broke off conversations to speak to them, the ton still bestowed them with smiles and acknowledgement.

Sarah relaxed and set out to try and enjoy the ball's grandeur.

"Miss Baxter," Lady Anita greeted, as she spied them approaching. "So glad you could come. Let me introduce you to my mama."

Sarah had never met a Duchess before, but the woman's warm smile and welcoming manner, very much like her daughter's, left her feeling accepted if not equal.

"Anita mentioned you are recently from Rome, Lord Stanley. Allow me to welcome you to London."

Richard bowed. "Thank you, Your Grace."

"Miss Baxter, would you care to take a turn about the room?" Anita asked.

"Yes, of course," Sarah said, and headed toward the open French doors with her. Guests mingled on the flagstone veranda that overlooked the home's extensive garden.

"I'm so glad Lady Cottlestone invited you tonight. I find that always meeting the same people in society can cause stagnation. It is so refreshing to have you as part of our set." Anita chose two champagne flutes from a tray carried by a passing footman and handed one to Sarah. "Oh, I do love pink champagne."

"I agree. It's a lovely beverage." Sarah chuckled as she took in the scene. Richard stood beside the Duchess in discussion, appearing relaxed and elegant. Others danced a quadrille, their gowns an assortment of vibrant colors. People mingled in groups discussing all manner of things, some casting inquisitive glances their way.

"Hmm, yes." Anita clicked her tongue. "See the lady arriving now, the one speaking to Lady Cottlestone?"

Sarah glanced toward the doors and nodded. The young woman was extremely tall and very elegant. Her silk gown fell from a figure made for a fashion runway. She was exquisite, but the distaste Sarah read on her face marred her beauty.

"That is Lady Patricia Meyers, Lady Cottlestone's goddaughter, and if the woman has her way, my cousin's future wife."

Sarah narrowed her eyes. Beautiful she might be, but she also appeared cold and uncaring. "I assume you mean the Lord Earnston is going to marry Lady Patricia?"

Anita scoffed. "She hopes to. You see, before his death, my cousin was betrothed to her. Their marriage was set for the end of this very season. But of course, the accident happened, and..."

Sarah knew exactly what Anita meant. At the sound of the quadrille winding down, she looked across the sea of dancers and met the surprised gaze of the earl himself. Heat washed her skin as she recalled their last embarrassing meeting. How was she to talk to the man without falling at his feet and apologizing profusely for his brother's death? Or babbling like a fool due to his good looks. Mentally, she chastised herself for being an idiot. What was she worrying about? No one knew hers and Richard's real identities and nor would they ever. If they kept to the plan, everything would work out fine.

"I do not believe Lord Earnston has any intention of marrying just yet," she heard Anita continue. "But Lady Patricia is determined and so, too, are my aunt and Patricia's mother."

"So they're not betrothed?" Sarah couldn't blame the

Earl for his decision. To marry your brother's betrothed just because he'd died didn't seem very romantic to her.

"No. I feel for Patricia, though. It must be awfully difficult to see the new Lord Earnston about London and at all society events."

"Why?" Sarah asked.

"They were twins, my dear. Had I not told you this?" Sarah nodded, feeling a pang of sympathy for Lady

Patricia. "I had forgotten."

Anita sipped her drink. "I will introduce you to Lord Earnston this evening. I am determined he make amends for his behavior."

"I look forward to it, but I don't want to be any trouble to his lordship," Sarah said.

"Nonsense, my dear. An introduction is no trouble." Sarah inwardly cringed. Would the earl be rude or pleasant? She deserved the worst of his temper after what she'd put his family through. Her hands started to sweat in her gloves.

"Are you well, Sarah? Would you care for some air on the terrace?"

"I do feel a little faint. Perhaps some fresh air will do me good."

Anita took her arm and led her outside toward the balustrade. The cool air was a welcome reprieve from the heated ballroom. Sarah took in the extensive grounds. Crickets clicked, and somewhere in the dark garden water trickled and flowed. She gripped the rough railing and drew calming breaths until her anxiety calmed.

"Lady Anita, are you going to introduce me?" rumbled the same voice that had ordered her to stop on that horrible night. She tensed, her muscles reacting faster than her mind could.

Yet tonight, instead of the hardened command, his

voice was deep and rich, pouring over her like chocolate on her tongue.

Anita spun about with a gasp. "Earnston, you scared me. Don't you know it is rude to sneak up on people?"

"Forgive me, cousin." He smiled, and Sarah once again reminded herself to close her mouth and calm her jitters. His lordship's dark blue eyes took in her features and gown, and Sarah wondered what he thought of her.

"Lord Earnston, this is Miss Sarah Baxter."

Sarah curtsied. "Good evening, Lord Earnston. It's a pleasure to meet you."

"The pleasure is all mine." His lordship smiled, and Sarah felt her insides flutter. So handsome and athletic, his strong, broad shoulders would draw the eye of any woman wishing to admire fine masculine art.

"Allow me to apologize, Miss Baxter, and make amends over my rudeness last evening. But I'm sure you will agree that strangers are not usually invited to one's entertainments."

Sarah refused to blush at this reminder of her mistake. "You have nothing to apologize for, my lord. I would have reacted the same in your situation."

The wind picked up, and the cool, refreshing breeze became chilled. Sarah rubbed her arms and pulled her shawl over her shoulders to ensure her scar remained hidden.

"Perhaps we ought to return indoors. Miss Baxter, would you do me the honor of the next dance? I believe it is to be a waltz."

A waltz. Most of the dances she had learned over the past two months had been easy, but she had not mastered the flowing steps of a waltz. Furthermore, it would make her nervous to dance with this man even were she accomplished. These two facts predicted a disastrous half hour.

"Of course," she found herself saying.

Anita moved toward the French doors, and Sarah took Lord Earnston's arm. He met her gaze, and all the warmth she had read in his manner a moment before was replaced with uncertainty, contemplation even. Mustering a smile, she stepped inside.

ERIC LOOKED DOWN AT THE ATTRACTIVE WOMAN LIGHTLY touching the crook of his elbow as they walked into the throng of dancers. She was tall for a woman and yet displayed elegance with every step, no awkwardness with her uncommon height. "I understand you're recently from Rome. How are you finding London so far, Miss Baxter?"

"Most interesting, my lord." She turned toward him. "How so?" The silk of her dress and the lush curves beneath sent heat spiraling through him. Eric pulled her closer than was necessary and swept her into the dance.

"London is very different from where we're from."

She focused on something over his shoulder, refusing to meet his eyes. Eric inwardly frowned and wondered why such a thing troubled him. Many times he'd danced and never bothered to converse with his partner. "Are you always so vague with your replies, Miss Baxter?"

She did look at him then, and Eric found himself grinning at her discomfort over his question. A rosy hue bloomed on her cheeks and made her more attractive than he cared to admit.

"No," she smiled. "I'm normally a very good talker. If you wish me to talk your ear off, I can certainly try."

Eric laughed, the sound unfamiliar to his ears. Was this the first time since William's death he'd found himself enjoying the moment? "What strange wording you use.

Talk your ear off—such speech must only be used on the Continent."

Sarah nodded, her expression serious. "Of course. Only on the Continent."

"I should imagine you have high expectations for your first season in London?" He noted that her green eyes darkened—but in displeasure or fear, he couldn't tell. He raised an eyebrow and fought not to smile.

"I'm not interested in marriage, my lord. I'm here to enjoy the delights of the season and that is all. I'm not looking for the season's delights to include a husband."

"You surprise me yet again, Miss Baxter. Not only was that not the answer I was expecting, but it wasn't vague in the least." He did laugh then and swept her into a turn, which brought forth her own chuckle. The delightful sound did odd things to his body. "Do you ride?" he asked, hoping she would say yes. She would look delectable in a riding habit among Richmond's or Hyde Park's trees and beautiful grounds.

"I do. I love to ride, although we have no horses stabled in town."

"Would you ride with me tomorrow morning? I have a mare that's placid enough for town." Eric held his breath for her answer. Why, he couldn't fathom. And at present he didn't want to delve into such musings. All that mattered was that he was dancing with a beautiful and intelligent woman. One he was attracted to not only physically but intellectually. He would have to thank Anita for resurrecting his association with Miss Baxter.

"I would like that, my lord. Thank you."

She smiled once more, and again Eric felt his breath seize in his lungs.

He swept her to a stop as the last strains of the waltz sounded. Regretfully, he bowed. "You waltz beautifully."

Her chuckle brought another smile to his lips. "I do believe you're in denial, my lord. I could think of a different word than 'beautiful' to express my dancing."

"I cannot." Nor could he. Miss Sarah Baxter was a breeze of fresh air in an idle society. She was an intriguing woman, and he wished to know her better.

He turned as Lady Patricia came to stand beside them. Anita trailed behind, a mulish turn to her mouth. He greeted his late brother's betrothed with a bow, then made the necessary introductions.

"Would you care to dance, cousin?" he asked Anita. As much as his brother had loved Patricia, he did not. It was better for all involved that he make himself scarce whenever she came into his sphere, lest he injure her further by denying their families' mutual wish for them to marry. Ignoring Patricia's disappointment, he held out his arm to Anita.

"I don't like country dances, Eric," she said, taking his arm anyway.

"Until tomorrow, Miss Baxter," he said, turning before he was out of her hearing.

"Tomorrow," she replied.

Eric smiled. It was already too many hours between now and morning.

"What has you looking so jovial, cousin?" Anita asked, a knowing twinkle in her eye.

"A good friend of mine once said, 'A gentleman never tells.'" Eric placed Anita in line and stepped back with the other men to commence the dance.

"How curious. And yet I do believe I know."

Eric laughed. "I believe you do."

SARAH ALLOWED THE MUSIC TO FLOW OVER HER AS SHE watched Lord Earnston dance and laugh with Anita. She had thought him handsome when serious, but now, smiling, talking, and laughing made him more devastatingly so.

She sighed in relief at having not tripped over her own feet during her waltz with the earl. He was a skilled dancer and had overcome her dancing inadequacies. The memory of him clasping her against his broad chest, his muscular shoulders that would be magnificent if ever bared for view, left her looking forward to the next time they danced. Never would she forget her waltz with a lord in nineteenth century

London. She would cherish the memory forever.

"I know what you're up to, Miss Baxter, and it will not work."

Sarah started and turned to face Lady Patricia. "I'm sorry. I don't understand."

"Your wiles are wasted on Lord Earnston, my dear. He is not for you."

Sarah beat back the urge to put the high and mighty Lady Patricia in her place. "Lady Anita introduced me to his lordship. That he danced with me I'm sure was his way of being polite. I have no interest in Lord Earnston."

"It would be a waste of your time. Our families are, at this moment, finalizing our wedding contract."

"Lord Earnston has proposed?" Sarah asked, pausing when she spied an older woman looking their way, her dark eyes hard and full of malice.

"Not yet. But he will. Lord Earnston always does what is correct. So you see, Miss Baxter, it is best not to form a tendre for his lordship."

Sarah bit her tongue and nodded. "I assure you I will not."

"Very good, and let me conclude by saying that I do

not believe it is appropriate for you to associate with Lady Anita. She is a duke's daughter, you know."

Sarah's eyes narrowed at the woman's implication that she was beneath such people. "Lady Anita is my friend, and one I will continue to see. Should Lord Earnston wish to speak or dance with me, I will not deny him as he seems a nice enough sort of fellow. If you have a problem with such facts, Lady Patricia, it is not my concern."

Sarah curtsied and walked away, grabbing a glass of champagne from a passing footman. The audacity of the woman! Had she not left at that moment, Sarah wasn't sure what would have come out of her mouth next. For all her angelic mien, blond hair, and alabaster complexion, Lady Patricia was the devil's spawn.

❧

"ARE YOU OKAY?" RICHARD ASKED, COMING TO STAND beside her.

Sarah filled him in on her conversation with Lady Patricia.

"She could be a complication we don't need," Richard said practically.

"Yes." Sarah added Patricia to her list of problems. "I believe I have an enemy."

"And an admirer, if Lord Earnston's besotted gaze is anything to go by." Richard elbowed her. "Don't worry — rumor has it Lord Earnston isn't interested in Lady Patricia."

"Gossiping already. How vulgar."

Richard laughed. "Vulgar, maybe. Amusing, yes." Richard pulled her toward a group of chairs and sat. "His lordship is unattached and looks to be for some time. And while you were dancing with him, I snuck out and did a quick search."

"Did you find anything?" Sarah asked, unable to disguise the hope in her voice.

"Lady Cottlestone's collection seems to sway toward furniture—pianos and pianofortes, to be precise. She has hardly any trinkets at all." Richard sighed. "Keep with the plan. We'll be home before you know it."

Sarah nodded, trying to keep the disappointment from her face. Keep with the plan. Simple enough, or perhaps not. Not when every time she was beside the delicious Lord Earnston, she had an overwhelming urge to beg his forgiveness and throw herself against him. Such specimens of men shouldn't be allowed in history. It didn't make a twenty-first century time traveling archaeologist's job at all easy.

And judging by the heated gaze from his lordship at this moment, he would be an easy conquest.

Sarah sculled the last of her champagne. What a conundrum.

CHAPTER 5

THE BOW STREET Runner flipped through his notepad, his pasty face pinched in serious contemplation. Eric wondered if he'd have been better off doing the job himself. The runner, for all his contacts, hadn't produced one ounce of information worth Eric's trouble.

"Lord Earnston, thank you for seeing me on such short notice."

Eric nodded. "From the missive I received, am I to believe you have procured a lead into my brother's death?"

"I have, my lord. A most promising one." The runner stopped on a page. "Last evening at the Cottlestone Ball, I was informed items in her ladyship's parlor were moved about and not returned to their original positions. Also, papers on her writing desk had been shifted. This, of course would not normally raise concerns, but as the room was off limits to guests, I thought it best to bring this to your attention."

Eric sat forward and frowned. "Lady Cottlestone notified you of this?" Blood raced through his veins at the possibility the culprit was finally back in town among them.

"I received a note this morning. I hope that was suitable, my lord. You did instruct your closest acquaintances to be mindful of anything out of the ordinary."

"Yes, that's fine." Eric tapped his fingers against his desk. "Could not a parlor maid cleaning up have done this?"

"That was a possibility, but her ladyship asked the staff who service those apartments, and all said they had not been into the room since yesterday morning."

"Hmm." Eric stood and walked to the window overlooking Belgrave Square. "No one saw anyone looking suspicious or acting oddly?"

The runner shook his head. "No. The staff was so busy with the ball, they didn't notice anyone out of the ordinary. But, if I may say so, my lord, it seems our killer is back in town."

Eric nodded, his attention on the unsuspecting populace outside his library window. "So it would seem," he said. "Now all we have to do is catch the baseborn whelp."

"We will. Sooner or later, they'll make a mistake, and this time, we'll be ready. You have my word on that, my lord."

Eric walked back to the desk and stood beside it. "And I'll hold you to your word, Mr. Simms."

The runner's swallow was audible. "Excellent." He stood. "I'll leave you now and update you when I have further news."

"Good day to you, sir." The short man scuttled off in haste. Eric then pulled open his desk drawer and lifted out the strange artifact.

He ran his fingers over the smooth metal casing. What

was it? He had no idea, but whoever wanted it was back to collect. A smile quirked his lips. They would not have the chance to disappear again. His aim would be better this time.

Deadly accurate in fact.

⁂

Sarah walked in to the breakfast parlor where a vast amount of food waited upon the sideboard. Ham, pheasant, eggs, toast, and chocolate, lovingly set out for them to choose. Sarah spooned some eggs on her plate and sat at the table.

No sooner had she taken her first bite of the fluffy eggs than Richard rushed in. She smiled at his ruffled hair and his haphazard attempt at tying a cravat so early in the morning. "You seem perky this morning, Richard."

Richard glanced at the footman, then dismissed him from the room. "If you keep using words like 'perky', the staff will start gossiping about you." He gave her a pointed stare and looked over the food.

"Ah, they won't say anything. You worry too much." Sarah poured Richard a coffee and then proceeded to fix herself a tea.

A footman entered carrying a silver salver. "A missive has arrived for you, Miss Baxter."

Sarah broke the seal and opened it. "Oh."

"What is it?" Richard asked.

"Lord Earnston cannot make our ride this morning. Seems he has an appointment he forgot."

"Oh, well, I'm sure the besotted fellow will ask you again."

Sarah absently tapped the letter on the table. It was

imperative he ask her out, if for no other reason than to obtain the device, yet she couldn't explain the sinking feeling of disappointment or the fervent hope he would wish to see her again just because.

"Well, I might head down to Bond Street then. There's sure to be an antique or an art shop among other specialty stores in the shopping precinct. Since I have no other plans for the morning."

"You're saying the mapping device may have found its way into a London antique store? Bit of a stretch, don't you think?"

She shrugged. "Doesn't hurt to look." It was possible Lord Earnston may have sold his brother's collection. She didn't really believe this was the case, but she couldn't fail getting it back again.

"Your father said the earl had the device, so you're wasting your morning. But," Richard paused, wiping his mouth with his napkin, "it's up to you, and like you said, it doesn't hurt to look. Do you want me to have the carriage brought around for you? I won't need it today, and it looks like a storm may be brewing."

"No," Sarah shook her head. "I'll take a hackney."

"I don't know if that's safe. Perhaps I should come with you. You don't have a maid."

Sarah waved Richard's concerns away. "I'll be fine."

"Take your mace at least."

"Not that I'll need it, but if it makes you feel better…" Thunder rumbled in the distance. Dammit, would nothing go her way today? It had started out such a lovely morning, but true to Richard's predictions, that was deteriorating by the minute.

"It would." Richard bit into his ham and sighed. "This is delicious."

"The kitchen staff can certainly cook a good breakfast," Sarah agreed, yet pushed her half-eaten meal away.

"I was starving after arriving home last night. Did you taste the awful food Lady Cottlestone had on offer at the ball?" Richard cringed. "The white soup nearly made me gag."

Sarah laughed. "I stuck to food I recognized."

"I should have as well," Richard said.

SARAH CHANGED INTO A GREEN SPRIG MUSLIN GOWN. THE morning's dry heat had turned heavy with moisture. She tied her bonnet ribbons beneath her chin and scrutinized her reflection in the mirror.

She didn't recognize herself. The twenty-first century woman was well and truly gone, and in her place stood a nineteenth century debutante. The dress was light and extremely flattering to her slender figure. Her dark hair was tied back with a ribbon, accentuating her cheekbones. It was like seeing an ancestor, not herself. Dismissing the image, Sarah grabbed the umbrella leaning against the armoire and headed downstairs.

Her carriage ride to Bond Street was quick, given their home wasn't far from the shopping precinct. The bustle never grew old. Some shopkeepers stood before their stores, trying to lure customers inside. Ladies strolled along the flagstone footpaths, their maids carrying their purchases followed close behind. A lad, covered in soot, ran toward a townhouse and dropped coal down the eye in the front of the home and into the underground storage vault.

A pang of sadness pricked Sarah's senses as she realized all these people in this special time were gone. Everyone she spoke to and observed. All long gone.

She gripped the seat as the carriage rocked to a halt. Then she opened the door, stepped down, and paid the driver. The shops ran along an alley and bore quaint wooden frontages with hand-painted signs.

Stores of every kind were available for those who had the means to buy. Milliners, shoemakers, jewelers, tobacconists, and haberdashers all showed off their wares in the windows. Sarah couldn't help but fall in love with the beauty.

Her first stop held an abundance of antiques and collectables. Furniture, games, glassware, and cutlery littered every available surface. If the device was here, it would be an awfully long search.

"Can I help you, my lady?"

Sarah spied the elderly shop owner peeking over a pile of books. She sauntered toward him. "Hello, yes. I collect peculiars. Do you have any to sell?

The old man nodded. "I do. This way if you please."

He led her toward the rear of the store to a row of glass-fronted cabinets filled with different and strange items. Thimbles, shrunken heads, gold chess pieces, and other unfamiliar items filled every space. Excitement and despair washed over her. Yes, she would be here for some time.

"Are you after anything in particular, my lady?"

Sarah smiled at the elderly gentleman and shook her head. "No, thank you."

The store doorbell jingled, and he hobbled away. She turned back to the cabinets, sighed, and set about examining the items.

"Miss Baxter?"

She jumped and turned to find Lord Earnston gazing at her with a quizzical brow.

Shit!

"Lord Earnston." She curtsied and watched as the earl took off his hat and ran a hand through his long, dark locks. The action held her captive. His arm flexed, showing off muscle hidden yet noticeable under his finely cut suit. Butterflies took flight in her stomach, and she touched her waist to calm her nervousness.

"Are you out to do some shopping?" She inwardly cringed at her pathetic question.

"I was on the street and saw you enter. Are you here alone?" He met her gaze, one eyebrow raised.

"Yes. Alone." She swallowed, realizing too late she'd forgotten to bring a maid.

"You are unchaperoned?" His accusing tone irked.

"As you see." She turned back to the cabinets, trying to ignore his presence filling the space. Better that than tell this high and mighty lord what he could do with his condescending inflection. The delight of seeing him lessened with the opinion she didn't care to hear.

He sighed and touched her arm. "Forgive me, Miss Baxter. I was merely concerned." He smiled. "This was my brother's favorite store. Whenever he came up to London, his first stop was always Bond Street."

Sarah nodded. "He liked antiques?"

"Yes, very much so. He collected peculiars in fact, and I'm gathering, since you're standing before cabinets full of them, you may also, Miss Baxter?"

"I do, although my interests sway to the rare and strange these days."

"I would love to see your collection, if you would allow it?" His lordship squatted and gazed at a collection of snuffboxes.

Panic assailed her, and she struggled to find words. "My collection is still to be packed and shipped from Rome. I should imagine it'll be here by the end of the Season."

"Excellent." His lordship summoned the storeowner and asked to examine a silver snuffbox with diamonds and etchings on its casing.

"That's lovely. Will you buy it?"

His lordship smiled and nodded. "I think so, yes."

"So you collect, as well?" She held her breath for his answer. To know he collected would at least eliminate her need to scrounge through every antique store in London and other people's homes.

"I do. I never liked William's hobby before, but since his death, I thought I owed it to him to continue his passion."

Sarah walked over to a tapestry sporting warring knights and ran her hand along the woven material. "I think that's admirable, my lord."

"Well," he shrugged, "it's no bother."

Excitement ran along her skin as she met his gaze. His intense study of her made it difficult to concentrate. "I'm sorry we could not ride this morning. I was looking forward to it."

"As was I," he said. "But an associate of mine could only meet me at that time. Would tomorrow suit?"

"Yes, of course." She smiled.

His lordship nodded and slipped his hat back on. "I should imagine you'll be bringing your maid this time, Miss Baxter?"

Sarah laughed. "Of course. I will not forget." She stood there for a time, regarding him as he completed his purchase and, with another nod, left the store. His physique automatically drew the eye, and her hands itched to touch him. What a shame she could only offer him friendship. Mentally, she shook herself.

What was she thinking? He wasn't some hunk she had met in a nightclub. Her orders were clear: she was here to find the device and get away from Lord Earnston before he discovered her identity. She was not here to indulge her lust.

wouldn't rest until the criminal was brought to justice. "Should she ever be caught, she deserves the earl's wrath."

"Yes, a wrath involving a hangman's noose. I cannot think of a more awful way of dying." Anita took a sip of tea.

A shudder ran through Sarah, and she set about turning the conversation to a more menial topic. The whole time they chatted of gowns, balls, and gossip, her mind remained a whirr of discord and worry. The earl had a Bow Street Runner on the case. They would have to be meticulous from now on. Richard's mistake could not happen again.

"Sarah?" Anita asked, touching her hand.

Sarah pulled herself from her thoughts. "Sorry, I was a mile away."

Lady Anita threw her a quizzical glance but repeated her remark. "Lord Earnston also informed me he is to ride with you tomorrow morn." She sat back on the settee and grinned. "I hope you comprehend how unpopular this will make you."

Sarah flinched. "Why? I thought Lord Earnston was a much sought-after gentleman in the ton." Had TimeArch missed some important tidbit of information on his lordship?

"He is one of the most eligible men in England, my dear," her friend said with a laugh. "And for the first time since I have known him, he has shown a marked interest in a woman. You."

Sarah stood and rounded the settee. "I'm sure he is merely being kind to his cousin's friend and nothing more. I promise you, by the end of the Season, his lordship's affections will be aimed elsewhere, and I will be merely a passing acquaintance." Although she couldn't stop wondering who Lord Earnston would eventually marry. Have a life with. Love…

"Lady Patricia mentioned you in passing." Anita stood and pulled on her gloves. "I should not tell you this as she is all but family, but I feel I should warn you."

Sarah peeked up from her intent examination of the settee's gold silk cover. "Warn me?"

"Yes." Anita walked over to her. "Lady Patricia will seek to cut you out of Lord Earnston's life. I doubt she'll allow anything to stand in her way of obtaining a countess coronet." Anita took her hand. "Do not appear so worried, my dear. For Lord Earnston to show interest in you is enough for me. I would love to welcome you as a cousin."

Sarah needed to put a halt to this direction of thought at once. "Anita, I'm not entering a war over your cousin. Lady Patricia can have him. I will, of course, befriend him, but nothing more. Please do not try and match-make." What a nightmare this Season would be if she had to contend with people trying to marry her off.

Anita grinned, and Sarah realized her friend was not listening to a word she said.

"I'm sure my cousin's powers of persuasion will win you over eventually."

Though Sarah doubted that, she smiled. "Are you leaving?"

"Yes, I must dash. Mama has a modiste arriving today. Next season will be upon us before we know it, and she wishes to be prepared."

SARAH WALKED ANITA TO THE DOOR BEFORE SEEKING OUT Richard. She found him in the upstairs parlor. "You asleep?"

Richard sat up with a start and rubbed his eyes. "I'm up."

"I hope so, because you'll never believe what I've been told." She flopped onto a chair. "It seems the other night when you went moseying about in Lady Cottlestone's home, you were not as stealthy as you should have been. Lady Cottlestone has informed Lord Earnston that someone has meddled in her private parlor."

"What!" Richard stood, his face paling. "Do they know it was me?"

"No. You were lucky this time. But I also found out that Lord Earnston hired a runner to investigate his brother's death." She sighed. "We'll have to be so careful from now on. If they catch either of us trying to find the mapping device…"

Richard leaned against the mantle, idly stroking the marble. "We'll lie low for a few balls, make them believe the felon has fled." Richard paused. "You need to get closer to his lordship and gain access to his homes and to him."

Sarah frowned. It wasn't easy starting a friendship with a man who filled you with guilt every time you were near him. For all his masculine charm—the long, mussed hair, his deep ocean blue eyes, and full lips—it was impossible to start a flirtation, no matter how much she lusted after him.

"I can't do it, Richard." She joined him at the mantle. "I killed his twin. He would kill me if he ever found out. It would be wrong of me to let him believe there's a future with me when there isn't."

Richard raised his eyebrows. "You will, and you know why. Because both our jobs depend on it. It is only a little flirting, after all. How much damage can you do?" He walked away waving his arms. "What happened to the independent, intelligent twenty-first century woman I know? You made a mistake—you did not kill his brother on purpose. And from this point on, I'll not hear another word about you feeling guilty and full of regret."

Sarah shushed him for fear the staff would hear. Richard growled and hugged her. How would she do the impossible? How was she to purposefully set out and deceive Lord Earnston again? "It's just so cruel. What if his lordship forms a tendre for me?" She stepped out of Richard's embrace. "Lady Anita is already matchmaking me to him, and Lady Patricia sees me as some sort of competition."

Richard nodded. "I understand where you're coming from, Sarah, but you know not to go against your father. Especially as we've already stuffed up more times than I care to remember. If Lord Earnston forms some sort of crush on you, it'll be short lived. Men of this era rarely married for love. You'll see when we go home and read about what happened to his family; his lordship would've moved on by the next season."

"What if we went to the earl and asked for the device. If we explain where we're from and apologize, perhaps he'll give it to us and let us go."

"And if he doesn't, what then?" Richard argued. "Are we to take guns with us and threaten him should he become difficult? No, we'll abide by your father's orders."

Sarah rested her forehead against the cold marble fireplace and welcomed the chill stone. "I can't talk of this now, I need to lie down. Don't forget we have Lord and Lady Connors' soiree tonight." Her feet dragged her toward the door.

"Keep your mind alert and free from guilt, and just do the job. For all our sakes."

She met Richard's gaze and recognized the fear in his

eyes. "I won't let us down. I don't want to end up dead any more than you do."

"As long as we're both on the same page," Richard said, lying back down on the settee and closing his eyes.

Sarah walked from the room. Stay on the same page, or write a whole new book? One without a happily ever after.

❦

ERIC COOLED HIS HEELS AND WAITED FOR MISS BAXTER to arrive at the Connors' soiree. His need to see her again was unusual for him and yet welcome. It had been such a long time since he'd felt anything other than hate and revenge. Perhaps there were other things in life to look forward to after all.

Like the woman walking through the ballroom doors at this moment. Eric relished the chance to admire her lithe form. The splendid gown of jade silk that he knew would accentuate the color of her eyes. Miss Baxter was a beautiful woman, and one he would like to know a lot better.

He hadn't planned on coming to the soiree and had all but resigned himself to only see her again at their ride tomorrow morning. But it wasn't soon enough, apparently, for here he was, his heart thrumming in expectation of the sound of her voice.

He took a long pull of his brandy and watched as Anita whisked Sarah away from her brother. He noted their direction before turning his attention back to Lord Stanley, carefully taking in the man's features. His skin was darker than hers, as if he'd spent too many hours in the sun. But that wasn't their only difference. The gentleman's hair was an odd shade of auburn. Nothing like his sister's ebony locks.

He started when a hand waved in front of him.

"Not your preferred sex, Earnston," Mettleston said, nodding toward Lord Stanley as he walked toward the card room.

Eric laughed. "Not my preferred sex ever. I was merely noting the difference between Miss Baxter and her brother. Odd that their hair and skin tones are so different. What say you?"

"I say, you need to drink that fine liquid in your glass and procure another. Perhaps Lord Stanley has spent more time outdoors or has the features of only one parent." Mettleston shrugged. "Who knows and who cares? Certainly not me."

Eric noted his friend's foxed state. "Care for a game of cards? With your current inebriation I'm sure to win," he said, trying to lighten his friend's sour mood.

"I care not. Drunk I may be, but idiot I am not." Mettleston gestured toward Anita and Miss Baxter. "See your cousin is here and has taken the Miss Baxter under her wing. Not two more beautiful women to be seen in society, I vow."

Eric's gaze snapped to where the two ladies stood, a bevy of beaus surrounding them, and couldn't agree more. Anita addressed Lord Kentum, and he realized it would be only a matter of time before the man asked for her hand. Kentum was as besotted as one ought to be when in love, and not the least afraid to show it in public.

Miss Baxter, on the other hand, stood to the side, more reserved but attentive to the conversation. Eric wondered what she was thinking, wishing to be privy to her most inner thoughts.

Mettleston chuckled. "I see your aversion to being in Miss Baxter's company has ended. Why, if you continue to stare at her in that way, you'll create talk."

Eric averted his gaze. "I was merely checking that Lady Anita is well and not suffering under all the suitors who skulk about her skirts."

Mettleston scoffed. "Liar."

Eric's lips twitched. "What has you in high dungeons, my friend?"

"Nothing a few more of these will not cure." Mettleston gestured with his glass, slopping some of its contents across the floor.

Eric turned toward a sudden burst of laughter and locked gazes with Miss Baxter as she came toward him with his cousin. Eric tried to keep his gaze from devouring her form as she walked, but his eyes stole over her like a wave over sand. He licked his lips, his mouth suddenly parched. After his less than gentlemanly perusal, he expected to see a becoming blush on her checks, but alas it was not to be. And she intrigued him more when she lifted her chin and eyebrows in acknowledgement of his appreciation. Eric's admiration for her doubled, and he smiled.

"Earnston, how unexpected to see you here. I did not think you were coming tonight."

Eric kissed Anita's cheek, but his attention was strictly on her companion.

"You look very well this evening, Miss Baxter," he said, keeping his attention focused on her. She curtsied, and he caught a whiff of her perfume, the scent of jasmine.

"Good evening, Lord Earnston." Miss Baxter glanced at Lord Mettleston, and Eric realized they'd not been introduced.

"Forgive me, Miss Baxter; this is my friend, Lord Mettleston."

She smiled at Mettleston and Eric felt suddenly ill at ease. Her smile, unlike so many gestures throughout the ton, was spontaneous and genuine and aimed at his friend.

"Miss Baxter, may I have the honor of the next dance? I believe it to be a waltz." Eric wondered what was wrong with him. His chest felt tight, his skin hot as if he were taken with a fever. Never had an answer mattered as much as this one did now. Why, he couldn't fathom; he only knew he had to dance with this woman again.

"I would like that, my lord."

And there was that smile again that made his breath catch and his heart thump. He took her hand, placed it on his, and led her out to the floor. Pulling himself to rights, he made an effort to act the gentleman.

Not the easiest thing to do when all he wanted was sweep her out the nearest exit and kiss her senseless in an utterly un-gentlemanlike manner.

CHAPTER 7

Sarah inwardly shook as she walked beside Lord Earnston onto the dance floor. If ever she had her chance to cement a friendship with his lordship, now was the time. Yet his marked attention, indicating an interest bordering on more than friendship, was hard to push aside.

She swallowed and turned to face him. His superfine coat felt wonderful under her hands, and the overwhelming urge to stroke the material almost won over her sense of decorum.

He held her just above her hip, and an exhilaration of desire shot to her core. She firmly fixed her attention over his shoulder and readied herself for the torture of the waltz.

And then they were moving, flowing and twirling around the dance floor between other couples. The turns were fast—dizzying, in fact. This time, however, Sarah was prepared and met each step with a little more grace than before. Excitement thrummed in her veins at being back in his lordships arms. To have his whole attention fixed only on her left her breathless.

She noted the other couples enjoying the dance; the gentlemen, so handsome in their satin knee-breeches and perfectly cut coats; the women on their arms beautifully dressed and the paradigm of Regency fashion; the gilded walls, enormous mirrors and magnificent artwork made the ballroom resemble a scene from a period movie. A wholly magical experience.

"You look," his lordship paused, catching her attention, "very beautiful, Miss Baxter."

"Is it customary, my lord, to praise so in society? Will you not be scolded should anyone find out you spoke to me in such a way?"

Lord Earnston smiled. "I will not tell if you do not."

Her gaze veered to his lips, and hers suddenly felt dry. Refusing to lick them, she took a calming breath instead. "Your secret is safe with me. And thank you for the compliment."

"You're very welcome." His gaze turned scorching. Sarah held back the squeak of alarm when he pulled her closer than he ought. She met Richard's gaze over his lordship's shoulder and noted his pleased grin. Well, she supposed he would be happy. Here she was, getting cozy with the lord with no effort on Richard's part at all.

"Did you end up buying any peculiars, Miss Baxter?"

She frowned. "Ah, no, my lord. There was nothing that caught my fancy."

"Was there not?"

Something in his lordship's tone gave Sarah pause. As if he was trying to get at something else. Was he flirting with her? Or was he suspicious? "No, but there are plenty of other antique stores in London. I'm sure I will find something among them that I'll like."

"I should imagine so." Lord Earnston pulled her into a

quick turn. Sarah laughed and gripped his lordship tighter. "Are you still free to ride tomorrow morning?"

"Yes," she said out of breath. "I'm looking forward to it."

"That would then make two of us."

Sarah deliberately ignored the double entendre hanging between them. It was merely her twenty-first century mind thinking dirty. "I have informed my maid, so you'll not need to scold me this time."

Lord Earnston grinned. "What a shame. I was hoping you'd buck convention and not bring one along."

Sarah refused to blink. "Liar."

"You know, Miss Baxter, you're the second person this eve to label me thus."

"Really?" she said, curious. "Can you tell me why?" Lord Earnston swung her in to another tight turn.

"Lord Mettleston believes—now prepare yourself to hear something quite shocking—I have formed a tendre for a lady here present tonight."

Sarah's heart raced. She bit her lip and wondered what the social protocol was when a gentleman shared such a personal tidbit. She was pretty sure she should tell him off and storm away. Yet all she could think was, did he mean her? And if so, what should she do with such a revelation? "Oh," was all she replied.

His lordship grinned. "I told him he was being absurd, of course, but then I have been known to twist my words."

Sarah held off the urge to fan her face and wondered if everyone else were as hot as she. Dancing in his lordship's arms, hearing his deep, rumbling voice was a challenge at the best of times, but when he aimed to make the woman in his arms melt like ice-cream on a hot summer's day, it was nearly impossible to stay composed. "You lie then," Sarah said, glad her voice came out strong and almost accusing.

Lord Earnston laughed. "Never lie, just…evade." He paused. "Are you not curious as to whom Lord Mettleston meant?"

"It would be silly of me to ask as I'm sure, because you are a gentleman, you wouldn't wish to cause me unease. You do realize women tend to look less than comely when flushed red to their roots. And you know how dedicated I am to finding a husband this season." Sarah smiled at her own sarcasm. But at least his lordship was being hospitable, and could well be on the way to counting her a friend, if such a thing were allowed in 1818.

He laughed. "Very well, I'll abide by your wish not to know, but you're wrong about a woman's flush. I believe there is nothing more beautiful than a delicate rosy hue on a woman's cheeks, especially after a pleasurable exertion."

Oh man he is hot!

Sarah said a silent prayer of thanks when the waltz ended and he swept her to a stop. "My lord, there is something—"

"My dear, you must introduce me at once to the lady who has kept you this past half-hour. I command it."

Sarah turned and found herself face to face with a formidable looking older woman. She dipped into a curtsy and then wished the ground would open up and swallow her. Why was it that whenever she was nervous, she forgot the damn etiquette rules? The curtsy was supposed to come after the introduction.

"Forgive me. Miss Baxter. This is my mother, the Countess of Earnston."

Sarah dipped into her second curtsy. "I'm very pleased to meet you, Lady Earnston."

"Well," her ladyship said, not responding any further. Instead, she pulled Lady Patricia forward and nigh threw her into his lordship's arms. "Dance with Lady Patricia, Eric. She is free this next set."

Lord Earnston bowed. "Until our ride tomorrow, Miss Baxter. Good night."

"Good night, my lord." Sarah curtsied.

When he didn't immediately move away, her ladyship gestured them to leave, and took Sarah's arm, adeptly steering her from the spot. Apprehension crept across Sarah's skin.

"Miss Baxter, I'm sure you're a very good sort of woman, but if you're seeking to marry my son, you're setting yourself up for misfortune."

Sarah noted her ladyship's cold eyes and immovable stance beneath the sweet voice and smiling mouth. "I do not wish to marry his lordship; I consider him merely an acquaintance, a friend, if you will, in society."

"A friendship between members of the opposite sex is an absurd notion. Such foolishness leads to folly, and you, Miss Baxter, will not lead my son to any such situation."

Sarah stopped and pulled her arm from her ladyship. "I have no desire to lead him anywhere." She caught sight of Lord Earnston enjoying his dance with Lady Patricia. They made a beautiful couple: elegant, tall, social equals. A pang of envy stabbed her, and she pushed it aside, breathing a sigh of relief when Lady Anita joined them.

"Aunt, lovely to see you tonight." She kissed her ladyship's cheek. Lady Earnston's features softened at the gesture, and Sarah caught a glimpse of a woman whose youthful beauty was still visible under the lines of time and spite.

"Anita dear, I have been talking to your delightful

friend, Miss Baxter. Patricia, as you can see, is dancing with Eric. Do you not think they make a fine couple?"

Anita didn't even bother to find them on the dance floor. "They make a lovely couple. As to whether they would match as a married couple, we should leave that decision to the respective parties. Don't you agree, Aunt?"

Sarah bit the inside of her cheeks to keep from cheering at Anita's kindly veiled warning.

"Ah, are my hopes of a match showing?" Her ladyship tittered.

Sarah inwardly laughed harder at the false modesty this society peahen was crowing about.

"Just a little," Anita said, smiling.

It was time for Sarah to untangle herself from this charged topic. "Well, I think they make a lovely couple. If you would excuse me." She curtsied to the older woman and headed off in the direction she had spotted Richard earlier. She exhaled a sigh of relief when she spotted him leaning on the card room door.

"We should leave." She turned and stared at the dancers. Lady Patricia caught her eye, and Sarah couldn't miss the smug smile her rival threw over his lordship's shoulder. She turned back to Richard.

"What's wrong?" he asked.

"They think I'm after him."

"Who?"

Sarah inwardly cursed. "Lord Earnston. His mother and Lady Patricia both think I want to marry him. Stuff this need to be careful for a week or two. Make sure when I'm riding with the earl tomorrow morning that you get into his home and investigate. The sooner we go home, the better."

Richard nodded. "And if I'm caught?"

"You won't be." The music ended, and the dancers

dispersed about the room. Lord Earnston bade a quick goodbye to Lady Patricia and departed her company.

An inner voice lauded his action, but Sarah quickly silenced it. She was not permitted to dabble with him. He was a means to an end, and that was all.

She would have to be more cunning if she wanted him to divulge the whereabouts of the mapping device. Cunning and creative—two words not normally associated with Sarah Baxter.

ERIC LEANED AGAINST A WINDOW FRAME AND WATCHED HIS mother storm across the room toward him. He stifled his annoyance. "Mother, what brings you to my side?"

"Do not play coy with me, Eric. You know very well why I wished to speak to you."

"Enlighten me," he said in a boorish tone meant to aggravate his maddening parent.

"What are you playing at with that chit Miss Baxter?" Eric glared at his parent. "You are overstepping your bounds, my lady."

"You are my son, and I may say and ask whatever I wish. Now, explain yourself."

"There is nothing to explain that warrants your attention." Eric took a sip of his whisky. "And you are forgetting the fact I am not betrothed to another."

"But you will be." His mother huffed. "How can you do this to Patricia? Why, just the other day, her mama spoke of the expected agreement between you two."

Eric couldn't have put it better. "Agreement" would be the sum total of the feelings he and Patricia would share if they ever married. She was a beautiful, young woman, and in desperate need of a coronet. Eric wasn't fool enough not to know what she sought in a marriage. It was a pity William never saw through her false motives.

"No one will tell me whom I marry, including you." He met his mother's heated gaze with one of his own. How she could even imagine him marrying the woman his brother loved was beyond him. He stemmed the urge to grind his teeth.

"Furthermore, what is this nonsense about riding in the park tomorrow? People will talk."

"Let them." He shrugged. "A ride in the park does not ruin a reputation." And there was no way he would miss riding with Miss Baxter.

"I will not have it. I warn you now, keep up this foolishness, and I'll never forgive you."

Eric bowed. "It seems we are in agreement." With a stab of regret, he sighed as his mother stormed away, the feathers atop her head flying around like a live bird. She was impossible, pigheaded, and downright vexing. He took a calming breath, and began searching the crowd for something to cheer him up, namely Miss Baxter. He spied her standing next to Lord Stanley.

Studying her, he wondered why she seemed different from the other women of his acquaintance. Why she fascinated him so. She dressed the same as other women. Was from a family of wealth and yet, somewhere along her path to adulthood, she'd blossomed into a woman of independent thought and ideals.

She was a woman who didn't follow society's rules, having said herself she wasn't seeking a husband. Which was agreeable with Eric as he wasn't looking for a wife. Yet, underneath the nerves he was sure he brought forth in her was a lady with a lot more plans and opinions, if only she'd open up to him. Miss Baxter was a delightful enigma, and she had him enthralled.

He glanced at her brother beside her. Again, the siblings' physical differences struck him. He frowned, but the puzzle wasn't nearly as intriguing as the anticipation of his riding appointment in the morning. It could not come soon enough.

CHAPTER 8

"Would you mind, Anita, if I walked outside for a moment? I'm feeling a little warm."

"Would you like me to join you?"

"No," Sarah said. "I need but a moment." She exited the room and welcomed the balmy night breeze. Walking to the edge of the terrace, she noted the lit lanterns throughout the garden.

The houses in present day London no longer had such generous, beautiful landscapes. Land was a rare commodity and soon sold off to make way for more flats in the city. Sarah took a deep breath and the scent of sandalwood wafted across her senses.

"It's lovely to see you again, Miss Baxter."

She'd know that voice anywhere. Lord Earnston stood behind her—a dark, overbearing shadow that skittered delicious vibrations down her spine.

"Thank you." He stepped beside her, and the action afforded her a glimpse of his profile.

"How did you fare after our ride this morning? Not too sore I hope," he asked.

Sarah smiled. "No. I am very well, thank you, my lord." She took a calming breath. After spending a fantastic morning with him, it was odd for her to be so nervous. Lord Earnston had opened up a little more about himself—his preference for country living over the capital, what plays at the theatre he enjoyed, and his political views. With every moment she spent in his company, Sarah liked him a little more.

She studied him as he stood next to her, his formal attire offered a different appeal tonight to the one he wore this morning. Not that he wasn't as devastating in buckskin breeches as he was in knee-high satin breeches. Both pants showed off his delectable backside very well.

Sarah leaned against the balustrade. What was it that made his lordship different from the many boyfriends she'd had in the past? Underneath the nineteenth century attire, he was just a guy like any other. Yes, he was wealthy and titled, but still a man. And yet, when she had his attention, she commanded it wholly, and he made her feel like she was the only woman in the world.

He turned, and she drank in his good looks. His chiseled cheeks and straight nose, lips that spoke with passion and thought. She wanted to kiss him and see what he tasted like. She cleared her throat. "Beautiful garden, my lord. Are all London establishments so lucky to have an oasis in their backyard?"

"Some, Miss Baxter." He smiled. "Would you care for a stroll?"

Sarah shook her head, confusion clouding her mind. The strong perfume of flowers surrounding the terrace tangled with his powerful presence. The heady mixture was further weighted by the unnerving fact they were alone. Very alone. "I should not?"

His lordship growled and pulled her along the terrace. "It is just a walk. I will not harm you."

"Very well," she agreed.

They ambled down the steps and walked along the gravel path and into the grounds as far as the lanterns' glow stretched. She stopped when the light gave way to shadow and sat at a stone bench just off the path. His lordship followed her and sighed as he came to sit beside her.

"I enjoyed our ride this morning, Miss Baxter. We should ride out together again."

Sarah crushed the image the word "ride" brought forth. She needed to get her mind out of the gutter. "I would like that, but I do not wish to cause trouble for you."

He ran a hand over his jaw. "I'm guessing you're referring to my mother. No matter what her opinions and wishes are, my life is my own, and I'll live it as I see fit."

"I do not doubt it. But I also believe your mother dislikes me." She turned toward him and again the seductive scent of sandalwood teased her senses. "I think she's warning me off."

He met her gaze, and her knees wobbled. Everything about him was alluring and charming, and under a moonlit night it was hard to control the temptation to lean forward and taste those firm lips.

"The question we should be asking is whether you'll be scared off?"

"I'm still sitting here, am I not?"

His eyes widened, and time seemed to still about them. The sound of the festivities dimmed as all she could hear was her own heart drumming. His lordship leaned in, gently brushed his lips against hers, and she was lost. It was wrong— so very, very wrong—and yet she couldn't form the words to halt where the slight contact was heading.

He seized her waist and pulled her against him. Sarah

lifted her gaze to his eyes, sparkling in the moonlight and promising nights of pleasure should she allow it.

"Are you sure you wish to do this, Miss Baxter?" His breathing was ragged.

"Call me Sarah." Her hands slid about his nape and pulled him down for a kiss. All thoughts of acting the debutante vanished when her lips touched his. Fire coursed through her veins as she gave into the kiss with abandon. His tongue danced with hers, sending her spiraling into a void of desire.

He growled, and Sarah shuffled closer. Needed to feel him, to touch the compelling man who was kissing her senseless.

No man had ever evoked such emotions from her before. Men normally ran a mile as soon as they found out what she did for a living. A boring archeologist wasn't going to turn into a siren in bed. And the men who thought her job wonderful were usually so boring it was an effort to stay awake throughout dinner. Then there were the gold diggers after her family's money. Though Lord Earnston didn't know what she did for a living, he did find her interesting enough to want to see her again, which was more than she'd experienced before.

His coat grazed her nipples, sending a dizzying sensation straight to her core. His hands ran down the back of her gown, and his kiss changed. Gone was the possessive heat consuming her, and in its place was warm seduction, an even more dangerous embrace. With every touch he bestowed, Sarah's skin burned, and she gave herself over to him, not caring about anything other than Lord Earnston and every delicious sensation he evoked in her.

He broke the kiss and pulled back, his heated gaze full of unvoiced questions and desires.

"Do you intend to stop, my lord?" She stroked his soft

hair, allowed her hands to graze his jaw and touch him exactly as she'd fantasized a few moments before. Well, not exactly. Still, he kept her held hard against him, his arms in no way lessening their clasp.

"No."

Sarah smiled and bit her lip at his deep, uneven response. A myriad of emotions crossed his face, and he looked like a man who'd experienced a profound life-changing incident, one she could easily identify with.

If his kiss could so unsettle her, she hated to think what sleeping with him would do…

She shivered.

"You're cold." He stood and pulled off his jacket.

Sarah allowed him to place the superfine garment over her shoulders. She pulled it closed with one hand and frowned at the heavy weight bumping her thigh. Curious, she reached into his coat pocket, and wrapped her hand around the object to pull it out. Her heart raced, and she blinked as she pulled out the entire reason for her presence in the nineteenth century.

She could have won an award for her portrayal of a calm, merely curious lady with her ticket home nestling in her palm.

Eric took the device and idly fiddled with it. "Strange, is it not?"

The object's silver casing caught the moonlight, and Sarah fought not to snatch it from his fingers and run. So, his lordship carried it with him. No wonder they couldn't find the damn thing.

"You don't know what it is?" she asked, gesturing toward the mapping device.

"No idea." He slid a finger over the smooth metal, and shook his head. "But I believe William's murderers do, and they want it back."

"May I take a closer look at it?" His lordship handed it over without qualm, and Sarah frowned, torn over her next move. Could she run fast enough to get away without him catching her? She noted the distance between her and the house. No. She'd never make it, and should he catch her, he'd know she was to blame for his family's tragedy.

"I've never seen anything like it." The lie lodged in her throat, and she hoped he wouldn't suspect her eagerness.

"It is one of my most cherished possessions." Lord Earnston took it back, and Sarah felt panic rise. She had to get the object in her possession for just a few hours, long enough to escape. Could she cajole his lordship into giving it to her as a gift? Yet she was reluctant to use their kiss to manipulate him. Such a low, callous act was unthinkable.

"Do you always carry it around with you?" she asked, unwilling to drop their conversation about the mapping device so soon.

"I do," he said. "When the murderers find the device, they'll find me and my waiting retribution."

She nodded, guilt clawing at her skin. "I hope you're able to move forward with your life one day. You deserve to be happy." She kissed him quickly. Pulling his jacket from her shoulders, she handed it back. "I think we should return before we're missed."

Lord Earnston slipped on his jacket and returned the mapping device to his pocket. "Yes, you're right." He took her hand and walked her back toward the terrace and the ball.

Let the games begin…

❧

THE NEXT MORNING, ERIC SAT IN HIS LIBRARY, MIND IN A quandary, body taut and unfulfilled. He gazed at the clock and debated if it was too early for a drink. He was thankful for the interruption when the door opened and his butler, James, walked in.

"My lord, Lord Mettleston to see you."

Thank God. He could use a diversion, not to mention a friend's opinion.

He poured two whiskies and returned to his desk as his friend strutted into the room.

"Earnston, there's talk of you all over town. And it's not past morn," Mettleston said without a word of hello.

Eric choked on his drink. "What about?"

Mettleston settled himself before the desk, a self-satisfied smirk on his lips. "How you were seen following Miss Baxter into the garden." He chuckled. "Care to enlighten me on the salacious details?"

Eric pinched the bridge of his nose. "If this blasted device," he said, throwing the strange peculiar onto his desk, "had not distracted us, I would have pushed to see just how far Miss Baxter's affections for me went."

Mettleston sat stunned, for once without a response.

"I kissed her," Eric said, "and I find myself wanting to do it again." He smiled at the memory. Had he kissed any of the other debutantes, they would have fluttered and fussed in their excitement. Not Sarah. She possessed a maturity he'd not seen before, not in women of her age in any case. He'd kissed her senseless, by God. She'd kissed him senseless, too, without dissembling into fits of the vapors or running to her brother demanding marriage.

Eric leaned forward on his desk. "Well, say something. It isn't like you to have no opinion."

Mettleston met his gaze. "What possessed you, man? She's unmarried and a debutante. Her brother will have your leg shackled to her before you know it if you keep up such antics." He took a sip of his drink. "Or he could take offense, and you may find yourself on a field of honor, staring down the barrel of a gun. And he'd have every right to shoot your scandalous arse, too. Unless, of course, you wish to marry her?"

"It was only a kiss. I didn't deflower her, Mettleston. And there were other couples walking the terrace and gardens. Just not where we were." Eric sighed and slouched back into his chair. "I don't know what's possessed me. Whenever I'm around the chit I can't control the need to touch her. Be near her. Listen to her." He paused.

Mettleston chuckled.

"What?"

"What indeed," the other man said. "So, the high-in-the- instep Earl of Earnston has fallen for a woman. I must admit, I had not thought I'd ever see the day. Congratulations; when will you ask for her hand?"

"Damnation! I have not fallen for her, and I'm not marrying anyone, let alone Miss Baxter. And you'd be wise not to start any such rumors. Last night was a slip of etiquette, that is all. I like her, and I believe the feeling is mutual. I like many women—it does not mean I'll marry any of them. And in any case, I never intend to marry, as you well know."

"I'm sure Lady Earnston would be happy to hear such words voiced aloud. And yet, you seem to be a little conflicted with your feelings toward this woman."

Eric couldn't meet the scrutiny of his friend's laughing gaze. Besides, his mind was too busy recalling Sarah and her slim, delectable form against his.

"Earnston, I am not going to ask what you are thinking. God knows I don't want to know. But you had better be careful. Talk is rife of your infatuation with the girl. If you do not intend marriage, you had better cool your ardor. Go see Mae. She'll set you to rights. And with any luck, put Miss Baxter out of your mind."

Eric gulped the last of the amber liquid and welcomed the burn down his throat. He doubted anyone other than Sarah would douse his desire for her. And now that he'd sampled her, he was not sure he had the strength to deny himself her affections. He wasn't ready for marriage, but perhaps if he worded his proposition correctly, Miss Baxter might be open to other delightful interludes…

"I'm off." Mettleston stood. "I'll leave you to ponder your thoughts. But take heed, Earnston—I'd prefer not to stand as your second. Although, of course, I would."

Eric smiled and came around the desk to escort Mettleston out. "Do not worry, I'll take heed. I promise neither you nor I will finish this Season with a bullet wound."

"I'll hold you to that promise."

CHAPTER 9

"Lord Earnston has the mapping device, and you're going to seduce him to get it back." Richard sat back in his chair, his breakfast forgotten before him, and stared at her with dismay.

"Yes. Exactly. I had it in my hand last night before he reclaimed it." Sarah bit into her toast and took a sip of tea as she outlined her plan, cooked up in the wee hours of the morning. Guilt be damned. It was time to go home without asking Richard to risk a bullet in his head trying to steal the device.

"You do realize you plan to prostitute yourself to gain this item. Does that not concern you?" He stood, pushed back his chair, and moved around the table to sit beside her. "I'm sure your father never wished you to do that."

Richard was right—her father would never condone such actions. But what choice did they have? The only time Lord Earnston would be without the device was when he slept.

And she couldn't see Richard climbing up his lordship's wall and stealing into his room late at night. "Father need never know what I do. And"—she shrugged—"Lord Earnston isn't ugly…"

Richard scoffed and threw her a dubious look.

"Well, okay, he looks like Henry Cavill, but in period. I'm sure my task at seducing him will not tax me too much."

"Only a few days ago, you were worried about hurting his lordship? And now you plan on sleeping with him. Do I need to remind you that such an action will cause a gentleman of this era to think you either a light skirt or after marriage?"

"I know what I said, and I haven't changed how I feel about my unforgiving past with him. But after last night and having the device in my hands, I know we cannot continue in this way. If I manage to get the device quickly, the less my leaving will hurt his lordship in the future." That is if his lordship cared about her at all. Their kiss said he did. Quite a lot, but perhaps it was only lust. Either way, she didn't need to stay any longer than they had to. Lord Earnston was such a gentleman, caring and thoughtful, that she could easily fall for him. And she wouldn't do that. He was not for her.

She pushed back her chair and stood. "I must get ready. I received a note from Anita this morning saying she had something she must discuss."

Richard took a piece of her toast and ate it. "What do you think it's about?"

"I have no idea, but I guess I'll find out soon enough." Sarah walked from the room, surprised her disclosure had gone so well. She had thought Richard would pitch a fit at plans to seduce the earl, especially as they'd only agreed to a little flirtation. The thought of doing just that assailed her mind, and she quivered. Inappropriate as it was, Sarah couldn't wait to start. It was time to turn this assignment into

an adventure.

※

ANITA ARRIVED FLUSH WITH EXCITEMENT DURING HER afternoon calls, and Sarah ushered her into the upstairs parlor, eager to hear what had put the ear-to-ear grin on her friend's face.

"You do realize you're the talk of the ton?"

Sarah dropped her cup into the saucer with a clatter. "Why?"

"People believe my cousin has formed a tendre for you. Of course, I am one of those people."

Sarah couldn't miss the self-satisfied smile on her friend's lips. "At a ball, people do take heed of what others around them are up to. But you did nothing wrong," Anita hastened to add. "Ladies are allowed to take the air."

She had taken a lot more than that. She took a sip of tea, hoping its warmth would account for her heated cheeks. Anita considered her for a moment as the silence stretched out.

"Perhaps it isn't only Lord Earnston who's formed a tendre?" she said finally.

A flutter raced through Sarah, as she relived the pleasant memory of Eric's lips devouring hers. She paused, mid sip, thinking of the glide of his hands across her skin, strong and intoxicating. Her cheeks burned.

"It's marvelous." Anita clapped her hands in excitement. "I couldn't have asked better for him. You'll do him a world of good." She wiped her lips with a napkin and met Sarah's gaze. "You know I had it from Eric himself today that he'll attend Lady Oliver's ball tonight."

Well, it shouldn't take long to put her new plan in action. "You're not backward in coming forward are you, Anita?"

Anita laughed. "I suppose I'm not, and what a wonderful saying. I've never heard it before. Is it from the Continent?" Rather than make up yet another cover story for yet another slip, Sarah rang the servant bell. "You could say that."

Still, she spent more time fiddling with the hem of her skirt as Anita chatted on about daily events in the life of the ton, awkwardly hinting for Sarah to ask her something. Try though she might, Sarah had trouble staying with the conversation and away from her thoughts of his lordship. In this society, it was paramount she keep her thoughts and feelings hidden behind a cloak of good breeding, no matter how false. Well, at least when she was in public. Behind closed doors, the earl was fair game.

Every time she closed her eyes, images of being locked with him in a far from decent embrace bombarded her. And they were utterly addictive. But she would have to ensure they were never caught lest she cause a scandal that ended with her married to a man born nearly two-hundred years before she was.

The footman entered and cleared away the tea, and Anita wiggled about on the settee, unable to sit still. "Well, if you aren't going ask, then I'll have to divulge it myself," Anita said, smiling. "This morning, Lord Kentum asked for my hand in marriage, and I've accepted him. We are betrothed!"

Sarah leaned across and hugged her friend. "I'm so happy for you. Congratulations."

"Thank you," Anita said, grinning from ear to ear. "I'm very happy."

"And so you should be. Lord Kentum is a keeper."

Anita frowned. "A keeper? What does that mean?"

Crap.

"It means, my dear, that he's smitten with you as much as you are with him, and you must keep him. Hence, he's a keeper."

Anita laughed. "I do love these foreign sayings. You must teach me more when we have time. But I haven't told you the best bit of my news."

"There's more?"

"Eric has offered his estate for a house party in celebration of my forthcoming nuptials. We're to leave London within the week and relax for a time down in Kent. You'll love that part of the county. Lord Stanley, of course, will be invited, also. Please say you'll attend. It wouldn't be the same without you." Anita paused. "I know we haven't known each other very long, but I do see you as one of my closest friends and would be honored by your company."

Sarah's heart stopped. Lord Earnston's home. Westerham. Kent. Could she travel back to his estate, live under his roof as a guest, all the while knowing she was the reason for the family's grief? And what if a local resident recognized her from the night she walked into the inn, sporting a gunshot wound? Her upper arm ached, and she rubbed the healed scar through the velvet of her riding ensemble.

"Richard and I would be the honored ones." She swallowed the dread rising in her throat. Seduction was one thing. A house party was a disaster.

SARAH DESCENDED THE STEPS OF THE CARRIAGE AND GAZED up at the imposing mansion before her. *Magnificent.* Large Roman pillars ran the full length of the home's facade.

Lights blazed from the multitude of windows and made the house sparkle on this dark, fun-filled eve. It was a vision she didn't want to forget.

The front doors bustled with guests lining up to enter. Was Lord Earnston gracing the gilt-edged walls within? A short few hours had passed since she'd last seen him, and yet it felt like an eternity. Her emotions warred between right and wrong, anticipation and trepidation over her plans with the charismatic earl. Could she pull this seduction off and still be seen as a lady in his eyes? Or merely as someone trying awfully hard to get him in the sack?

Richard took her arm, and they proceeded through the reception line before entering a room that would outdo the Royal Ballroom at Richmond Palace.

Mirrors and the golden and silver silk wallpaper bounced light and color throughout the grand space.

"This is a sight you don't often see," Richard said, meeting her gaze.

"You can say that again. It's spectacular."

Anita waved from the throng and headed over to them. Sarah curtsied, and Richard bade them goodbye before heading to the card room.

"I'm so glad you've arrived. Come, Lord Kentum is near the terrace doors." She wasn't even subtle about steering them toward him. Although, Sarah had to concede, his lordship did appear very dashing in his eveningwear. She curtsied when they joined the marquis's set and swiftly fell into easy conversation with his friends.

A footman offered her a glass of sickly sweet Ratafia. She declined and instead grabbed a glass of champagne. She took a sip, her attention on the guests before she spotted Lord Earnston some distance away. Who could miss such a man? He effortlessly out-classed every other gentleman there, rendering them all nondescript. Her gaze took in his appearance, and her breathing hitched.

His coat fitted him like a second skin, showing his toned arms and broad shoulders to perfection. Was he so unaware of the stunning sight he made? His nonchalant stance only accentuated his latent sexual prowess. A prowess Sarah had had the delight of experiencing. Her body thrummed at the memory, and she opened the fan hanging from her wrist and cooled her cheeks. Fashion accessories from the nineteenth century did come in handy.

She tore her gaze from him, lest he catch her ogling him like the sex-starved woman she was instead of the innocent virgin she showed to the ton. Determined, she kept her focus on the dancers and the guests circulating the room.

She frowned as she began to notice the many ladies present casting seductive, veiled glances toward the Earl. Taking a sip of her drink, she peeked over her fan to see his reaction. He was ignorant of such ogling. His lordship had not the foggiest idea what effect his presence in a ball-room had on the opposite sex.

She knew precisely what effect he had on her. It was like having an electric charge fire her blood. That was a constant since her first glance of him. Now, her soul begged to fall victim to his silent charms.

His lordship grabbed a second glass of brandy from a waiting footman and drank it down in one swallow. A trickle of unease pricked her senses. Was he drunk? She watched with growing concern as he commandeered yet another brandy and downed it as well.

Why did he want to be intoxicated? An appalling thought crossed her mind. Was he so embarrassed and regretful over their actions, he was afraid to face her without fortification? How embarrassing—and not at all helpful when she planned to seduce him.

Perhaps he was to expose what they had done? He certainly appeared tense, his face aloof and not at all welcoming.

She choked on her drink as his gaze met hers like a physical blow. His dark, sinful gaze roamed her form, and a satisfied smile lifted the corners of his mouth. Goose bumps rose over her flesh, part thrilled and part nervous, and Sarah tried to get her emotions under tight control. She smiled when the blasted man had the audacity to wink at her before taking another glass of the intoxicating liquid he had a penchant for tonight.

The master of ceremonies announced the first dance and, much to Sarah's amusement, a dashing figure bowed before her.

"Kentum, please do the honor of introducing me to your delightful company." Lord Dean grinned, and Sarah found herself laughing at his light-hearted flirting.

His shirt collar was far from starched. His clothing, although clean, was in need of a good iron. Dandy extraordinaire, he definitely was not. His hair was unkempt, sun bleached, and scraggly. It was easier to imagine him surfing Bells Beach in Australia than dancing away the night in nineteenth century England.

"May I have the next dance, Miss Baxter?"

Sarah nodded. "Of course." He walked her out onto the dance floor and pulled her into his arms for a waltz.

"I do believe I am the object of every gentleman's jealousy in this room at present, Miss Baxter."

Sarah remained amused at his open manner and saucy words. The smile faded fast, however, as it dawned on her what he was truly after. "You tease, my lord. If anything, they are jealous I'm dancing with a future duke," she said, attempting to draw some boundaries.

His eyes smoldered. Sarah swallowed her annoyance that he wore the same expression Lord Earnston had in the garden, as if she was a delicious morsel to be devoured.

"You do yourself disfavor, Miss Baxter."

He yanked her close for a turn. How many men were going to try to pick her up in nineteenth century England?

And just what did one say to a randy partner that would not get her thrown out of this party, too? She played it safe and said nothing.

"Can you not feel a certain earl's eyes upon us, Miss Baxter? If the fellow could draw a sword, I'd be dead." He laughed as his hold increased for the coming turn—or to annoy Lord Earnston, Sarah wasn't sure.

But she knew her game and refused to react to or acknowledge the truth of his words. She knew Lord Earnston was watching them. His stance against the wall might have appeared relaxed, but his face proclaimed something else entirely. And, for some ridiculous reason, she liked it.

The dance ended, and Lord Dean glided her to a stop. He bowed over her hand. "Thank you for a wonderful waltz, Miss Baxter. I can only say how sorry I am that I did not meet you first."

"Thank you, my lord; it was most enjoyable. I hope we may have the chance to do it again someday."

Lord Dean's eyes searched hers, once again setting off stalker alarm bells in the back of her mind. She raised her brows and refused her mouth's urge to tell him to take a hike.

"That, Miss Baxter, you can count on. Until the banns have been called, a gentleman must never give up hope."

CHAPTER 10

"Excuse me, Miss Baxter, the Duchess of Winters wishes to speak with you. May I escort you?"

Sarah started at the blunt question from behind. She turned and curtsied to Lord Earnston, who loomed over her like a portent of doom.

"Of course." Sarah took his proffered arm. Why was he so annoyed? "Is something the matter with Her Grace?" She tried to locate Anita's mother.

He glowered, his body taut as a bow string, and continued walking silently through the masses. So, he was angry with her. Sufficiently so that he was about to give her a set down. She tightened her grip on his sleeve, reveling in the muscular perfection under his eveningwear and the argument that was about to ensue.

He whipped her past potted palms hiding a doorway and into an abandoned passage. Wall sconces cast minimal light as his lordship continued to pull her along the Aubusson rug running its length. He paused and checked the passage before escorting her into a room to one side.

Tapestries hung from the walls, and needlework in all its forms lay scattered on chaise lounges, chairs, and settees.

"My lord, I do believe we've taken a wrong turn at some point, as it seems Her Grace is not present in this sewing room." She couldn't resist getting in the first volley. "Unless of course," she continued, "Her Grace is foregoing the delights of the ball to sew, and is hidden somewhere under all this mess." She bit back a laugh as his lordship's scowl deepened.

But her heart sped up as he snicked the bolt on the door into place. He lit a cheroot and leaned against the door, taking just one puff before he ambled to the hearth and threw it onto the empty grate. His dark hooded gaze resembled that of a predator about to attack. For the first time in her life, Sarah could relate to Little Red Riding Hood as she was about to be gobbled up by the Big Bad Wolf.

She swallowed.

"Did you have a pleasant waltz, Miss Baxter?"

She lifted her chin. "Why, yes, I did as a matter of fact. Lord Dean is very…personable." Lord Earnston stalked around the settee and stood before her. He stared down at her, and it took all her control not to smile at his jealousy.

It was obvious he was trying to scare her, ride roughshod over her, but little did he know she was never one to sit back and take anything anyone meted out. Best to lay the ground rules now and not later.

"Are you toying with me, Miss Baxter?"

He stepped closer still, and his breath caressed her lips. They were so close—only a slight lean away. Sarah swayed forward to brush her lips against his, and her insides rolled in a delicious slide. "No," she whispered.

He growled and yanked her hard against his chest. She grinned and ran her fingers through the hair at his nape.

His breathing came in short, ragged gasps that matched hers.

"Where did you come from?"

Pain tore through her at the truthful answer she should give him. But she had to evade the question. "From the same place everyone does." She paused, grinning. "Why, their mother of course."

"You're a teasing little minx." His lordship smiled. "Will you call me Eric when we're in private?"

Sarah nodded. "I'd like that."

"So would I," he said and kissed her. Hard.

Liquid heat poured through her, and she reveled in the demanding, impassioned embrace. Like their previous encounter, his kiss sent her spiraling into a vortex of delight. He pushed her gown from her shoulder and nipped at her bare skin. She leaned back and welcomed him to slide his tongue over her flesh. His hand cupped her breast, and she whimpered her need for this, for him.

How was it possible to feel so much desire for a single person? And why with a man born two-hundred years before her? A saying her father quoted often floated through her mind. *When lightning strikes, you should always follow your heart, not your head.* He found her nipple through her gown, pinched the pebbled flesh, and she lost all train of thought.

Grabbing his chin she pulled him up for a kiss. Oh, she wanted him. Wanted him to take her here in this cozy sewing room and damn the consequences. He lifted her and strode to a table beside the couch.

He grappled behind her, and she heard the contents of the table scatter across the floor. His hand lifted her gown and cool air kissed her legs. He stepped between her thighs and the rigid length hidden by his trousers grazed her skin.

Sarah gasped as he pushed against her undergarments, teasing her with his size and hardness.

Eric pulled back and stared down at her, his eyes pools of fierceness and need.

"Tell me to stop."

She ran her hand up the lapels of his coat and felt the outline of the mapping device in one of his coat pockets. She pushed his jacket off his shoulders and let it fall to the floor. "I can't."

His hand slid up her leg and touched her. Sarah bit her lip as he rubbed and teased her heated flesh. Their gazes locked, and she whimpered when he took her lips, his tongue mimicking what she wanted him to do with another part of his anatomy. Especially where he touched her now...

Laughter sounded close by and they froze. Eric growled and stepped back, his gaze on the door. Sarah slid from the table, hastily pulling at her neckline and righting her skirts, straightening them as best she could.

Eric turned and silently regarded her. "I think they've gone, but I should return you to the ball before you're missed."

Sarah walked over to a mirror hanging on the wall. Her skin was flushed, her lips red and swollen. She bit them and wondered how she could return looking like a woman thoroughly manhandled.

She pinned a stray lock of hair back into place and fought her desire to have him anyway. "You go. I'd like to stay here a moment."

He came and stood behind her and kissed her neck. Goose bumps lifted on her skin. It would be so easy to lean into him, let him feel her response and desire to continue what they'd started.

"Good night, Sarah."

He picked up his coat and left. She collapsed into the settees' soft cushions. She fanned herself with her hands and hoped she'd soon cool down. Damn. His coat fell, but the device didn't. She couldn't even claim that as a balm for her frustration. That was her ticket out of Kent, so to speak. Talk about stuffing up royally! Yes, she was playing with fire, and she had the definite sense she would be the one who ended up getting burned.

ERIC STRODE TOWARD THE SIDE EXIT AT THE END OF THE hall. The cool night air pricked his skin, and he welcomed the temperature change. Never had he ever been so close to deflowering a virgin.

"Christ," he swore, running a hand through his hair as he rounded the front of the London home. He'd wanted to possess her, make her his in the most basic form. A tremor rocked him, and he called for his carriage. Hopefully, he could escape before someone found him in this state. Hard. Unfulfilled. Hungry, and not for a repast.

His carriage pulled up. Calling for home, he stepped inside and threw himself onto the squabs in the dark, calming interior. The carriage weaved its way through the Mayfair streets, and he gazed absently at the houses, not seeing any of them—only the woman he'd left in a sewing room, tousled and kissed within an inch of her life.

She was marvelous.

He'd not thought to feel anything again after his brother died. And now that he did, it was a heady emotion and not one he wished to live without.

He gripped the leather strap as the carriage rounded a corner. So what was his next move?

Court her like the gentleman he was raised to be and

run the risk of another man capturing her heart? Or seduce her and make her marry him as a guaranteed consequence? Both were tempting. The carriage rocked to a halt before his home. He stepped down and strode to the door, opening it himself and startling the footman still making his way toward the threshold. Eric passed him his hat and coat and headed for the library to pour himself a brandy.

He would do both. Court Sarah and seduce her at the same time. She had ignited a fire in his soul, and he could no longer live without her.

He shook his head. He was a doomed rake. A man in love.

CHAPTER 11

SARAH SPIED the invitation sitting on her plate, recognizing Anita's flowing script immediately. She read the short note and then met Richard's expectant gaze.

"Anita has invited us to her betrothal party at Lord Earnston's estate in Westerham," she said as she picked up her plate and strolled to the sideboard to choose her breakfast.

"And are we going?"

Sarah shrugged and tried to appear nonchalant. "What choice do we have? I've also accepted the invitation to a masquerade ball this week."

"I noticed you missing for a time at Lady Oliver's ball." Richard's eyebrow rose. "Remarkably, Lord Earnston was also absent."

She managed to suppress her grin at this quandary. "I'm only doing my job," she said.

He scoffed. "Keep telling yourself that. You never know—you might actually start believing it."

They ate in silence for a time, lost in their own

thoughts, Sarah's on a certain rakish earl who stole her breath and her sanity with just a touch.

Heat bloomed on her cheeks.

Richard pushed his plate away. "What are you going to do when he asks you to marry him? Men of his station don't dally with debutantes without marriage as their ultimate goal."

Sarah took a sip of tea. "Don't be ridiculous. Marriage is the last thing Eric would be thinking about."

"That's where you're wrong. You're thinking with a modern woman's mind, not as an early nineteenth century miss. Trust me, he's thinking of rings and vows. Are you prepared for the consequences when he asks for your hand and receives a no as your reply?"

His exasperated expression sobered her. "I feel a headache coming on." She rubbed her temples. "But we can't go back to Plan A or you stealing the device."

"No." Richard shook his head. "You've started this game, and you'll have to play it to the end. But just make sure you take the device at the first opportunity. Time is running out." Yes it was, and the thought left her empty. Back in the present day, she didn't even have a boyfriend. For that matter, she hadn't slept with a guy in more than twelve months. And here she was in 1818 with a delicious lord chasing her skirts. What a difference two-hundred years could make to one's dating life.

"I'll get the device as soon as I can without being obvious. I promise."

Richard sighed. "For your sake, I hope he intends to just dabble with you after all."

Sarah faked a grin to ease his concern. "I'm all for dabbling." He laughed and left the table. Her smile faded as the breakfast room door closed. "Dabbling" didn't sound at all appealing anymore.

⚜

SHE WAS CHAPERONED TO THE MASQUERADE BALL BY THE Duke and Duchess of Winters after Richard declined the invitation, citing he needed a night off from highly starched neck cloths and sickening perfume. The duke himself was chatty and jovial in the carriage, speculating over the entertainment to come.

The carriage rolled to a halt before Sarah's first glimpse of a London ducal address. Rich didn't describe how wealthy Lord Dean's family must be.

Anita gazed out the window, not an ounce of awe to be seen, while they waited for her parents to alight.

"I've never seen anything so grand." Sarah stepped down and basked in the grandeur. The property even boasted its own front drive with sweeping steps leading to the front double doors.

They greeted their hosts in the foyer and headed at a dignified pace toward the ballroom. There Anita bid her parents farewell and beckoned Sarah into the throng to join her set of friends. Sarah loved the carnival atmosphere, a very close comparison to Mardi Gras in New Orleans. Some dressed like her in a dark domino, others as characters of plays or Greek gods. Despite her dilemma, tonight promised to be fun.

Lord Kentum was easy to find, since he had dressed as the God Eos to match his newly betrothed's Tithonus. Sarah smiled at the striking pair they made, robed in matching saffron.

Lord Dean's ballroom shone with hundreds of lighted candles, some covered in colored shades, creating a modern party-light effect. The terrace tonight would serve as an extension to the ballroom to accommodate the crowd. White paper lanterns hung along the terrace pergola, and hundreds more were strategically placed in the trees beyond. The supper room, positioned off the main ballroom floor, was loaded with an array of foods to tempt any palate.

Sarah studied the pyramids of crayfish, sandwiches, and asparagus and didn't think they looked too bad. But seeing animal tongues and soup with weird floating things on top made her wish she could walk into a McDonalds and order a burger.

The ladies eventually stopped near the terrace door, the cooler, tempting air kissing Sarah's skin. Lord Dean spied them and strolled over, smiling.

"How extravagant and beautiful you are tonight, Lady Anita. Miss Baxter. Had Lady Anita been wearing a mask, I would never have located you." His lordship met her gaze, and Sarah noted the heat behind his words.

"Sarah is more exotic than I," Anita declared, clasping Lord Kentum's arm.

Sarah laughed. She did feel very different, dressed in her black and white Venetian inspired domino. Her ebony feathered mask concealed her face well, only allowing her lips to show. Her maid had piled her hair into a curled motif atop her head, then powdered the entire creation before adorning it with colorful ostrich feathers strategically placed throughout. The design hid her coloring to perfection, leaving her feeling seductive and foreign.

But it was just her luck she couldn't think of an out when Lord Dean offered to give her a personal, guided tour of the public areas set aside for the ball. She grew uneasy under his marked attentions. His constant flattery and excessive courtesy were becoming obvious, and drawing not a small amount of scrutiny from the gathered ton.

If that weren't uncomfortable enough, she soon spotted

Lord Earnston also strolling the lawns, Lady Patricia hanging from his arm, her smile bright and her laughter braying as his lordship led her about the guests.

Sarah's gaze slid over him like a caress, taking in every little detail. He wore no mask; instead he had opted not to shave, and a dark shadow marred his jaw. His hair, too, was messier than normal—rather how it appeared after their first kiss. He had an air of mystery, danger, and so damn untouchable in his domino that physical pain tore through Sarah's chest. Her cheeks grew warm as she wondered how much clothing Eric wore under his concealing cloak.

Lady Patricia stretched up to whisper something in his ear, the two looking for all the world like an easy, married couple.

Sarah dismissed her jealousy as redundant—she was here to do a job and one job only. It was best if Eric did form an understanding with Lady Patricia. He had to marry someone after she left. For all Anita's voiced concern that the two were not suitable for one another, Sarah disagreed to an extent. They were social equals and had known each other all their lives. And Lady Patricia was from this time.

Sarah was not.

She tore her gaze away from the pair and turned her attention to Lord Dean. He passed her a glass of champagne, and she smiled her thanks before taking a large sip.

"Do you like my home, Miss Baxter?" he asked as they joined the group huddled about Anita.

Sarah nodded absently. "Very much, my lord."

"I'm so glad you approve." He lifted her hand and kissed her glove. Sarah took another sip of her drink, not really sure what she should do in response. Wiping the back of her hand on her dress probably wouldn't earn favor with the ton.

Lord Kentum picked that moment to ask Lord Dean a question, and the rake turned his marked attention elsewhere. Sarah silently thanked Anita's betrothed for the reprieve.

Like a moth to a flame, Sarah sought out Eric once more. Well, who could resist a six-foot tall gentleman made of solid muscle hidden beneath a cloak like a delicious piece of sweet meat?

"What do you say, Sarah? Would you like to join us?" That depended entirely on what Anita's original question had been.

Focus, Baxter.

"Where are you going?"

"Lord Kentum wishes to see the pond, and Lord Dean has agreed to accompany us. Would you like to join us?" Anita asked.

"I'd rather stay here if that's all right." At least standing in place would cut down on her conversational mistakes tonight.

Anita kissed her cheek and took Lord Kentum's arm. They soon disappeared into the wooded gardens, and Sarah helped herself to another champagne flute to bide her time.

She ambled through the gardens, gazing at the fragrant flowerbeds. Crossing beneath a large oak tree, she looked toward the home. Hidden from view, she watched the famous ton in all its glory, stamping the details into her brain to remember for the rest of her life.

She tried to make out Eric among the crowd but couldn't find him. Where was he? Or more importantly, what was he up to? She spied Lady Patricia talking to Lady Earnston, the displeasure on their faces obvious. Sarah frowned and wondered what they spoke about. "Nothing good I imagine."

"Did you say something?"

Sarah gasped, startled by the husky voice behind her. Eric stepped into a spot of dappled moonlight, and she stared, speechless, at the virile, delectable man. His scent of sandalwood intoxicated her senses more than champagne. Her gaze traveled down his form and heat pooled in her belly.

He smiled and leaned nonchalantly against the tree. She steeled herself to remain strong and not start drooling.

"Good evening, my lord."

"We're alone, Sarah. I thought we agreed to use our first names."

She nodded, peeking over her shoulder to ensure their privacy. "So we did." Masquerade or not, she could not be caught alone with him in such a secluded location. "How long have you been standing here?"

His teeth flashed in the dark, and a deep chuckle preceded the smile. "Long enough." He took her hand, pulling her toward him in the dark. "You are beautiful tonight."

Sarah's heart sped up at the sweet gesture. "Eric…"

He cradled her face in his hands, and Sarah fought to breathe. His touch sent her reputation catapulting toward social ruin. "What, my dear?" He leaned down and kissed her.

Sarah shut her eyes and reveled in the chaste embrace. What was he doing to her? His thumb sensuously caressed her earlobe, delivering a delicious tremble in its wake.

"We shouldn't be doing this." Of course she should be doing this—it was better this way for everyone. Richard was less likely to be killed if she seduced the earl and took the device after a night of wild, passionate sex. But who was she kidding? Whatever she felt for Eric had long ago changed from a means to an end.

Inwardly, she swore.

"Tell me why we should not." He untied her mask ribbon and let the facade drop.

"I don't want to hurt you." And that was one remark she did mean. She never again wanted to see the pain in his eyes the night his brother died.

"You could not." Eric brushed his lips against her neck, eliciting a sigh from her. "Kiss me," he whispered against her ear.

She turned, and their lips touched. Meshed. Held. The kiss ignited a whirlwind of flame. She matched his brazenness with every touch, every glide of tongue against her own. Want and need overtook all good sense, and she fought not to lose all control and let him take her up against the tree.

It was madness, this overwhelming feeling of rightness between them. His hands slid to her waist and cupped her arse. She gasped as he pulled her into him, his desire for her hard against her belly. She clutched at him, trying to hold onto a semblance of decorum.

But with every moment the kiss continued, self-control surrendered to need. He picked her up and walked deeper into the trees until she was, indeed, pressed up against an old oak. Dear God, she couldn't make love to him here! In a garden and at a ball.

Then Eric pushed his heat between her thighs, and Sarah couldn't think of anything she wanted more. Social etiquette and her conscience be damned. To have him want her with such ardor was the most intoxicating elixir she'd ever known. And he was just as addictive.

Air cooled her leg, and she realized his hand was high on her thigh, stoking her heated skin and coming painfully close to her core. She mumbled her acquiescence and kissed him hard. Eric moaned and ground against her. "You're mine."

She met his heated gaze and tried to calm her pounding heartbeat. "Eric…"

"Don't say anything. I know what I want." He paused. "I want you."

He kissed her again, and her heart melted to the unrelenting charm and reverence she felt in his embrace. She refused to acknowledge there was anything other than physical desire between them, that she shouldn't feel anything for the earl. Regency England rakes didn't fall for debutantes. His soft lips moved over hers in a dance of seduction, and she waltzed, unable to take heed of her own warning.

He clutched her face and tipped her chin to deepen the kiss. His fingers speared through her hair and knocked feathers and pins from their set. She relished the delicious feeling in her soul only this man had ever stirred.

"Marry me, Sarah."

Sarah gaped as the shock left her floundering, trying to form words.

"I know we have not known each other long, and you may think I'm being too forward. But I know who I want as my wife. Please say you'll marry me and become my countess."

Sarah wiggled out of his embrace and stepped aside. He couldn't have asked what she thought he had. Stunned, she searched for something to say, anything. Still words failed her, her vocal cords seizing into knots. And in truth what could she say?

I would love to, but I'm sorry, my lord, as I'm not from your time and will not be staying beyond the Season. And then, after I've stolen from you, I will leave you again without answers or closure.

Tears blurred her vision. She was going to hell for sure.

"Eric, I... You see..." Had she been born in this century, she would have already said yes.

But she had not.

The sound of voices floated up from the direction of the pond. Sarah threw a panicked look toward the shadowed figures emerging from the trees. Eric growled and stepped away. She quickly fixed her hair and pulled her domino hood over to cover what she'd missed. Her mask was nowhere to be found.

Lady Anita walked beside Lord Kentum, her animated conversation cutting through the night. Lord Dean ambled behind, his gaze on the path ahead. Sarah called them over, hoping they wouldn't pick up on the shakiness in her voice. She cast a glance at Eric who stood glaring at her friends. "There you are, Miss Baxter. I was wondering where you might have wandered to."

Eric tensed. "Not far, as you can see."

Sarah smiled to hide her unease. Lord Dean eyed Eric suspiciously.

"May I escort you back, Miss Baxter? Supper is about to be served."

"I think not, Dean," Eric said. The words dripped with bored nonchalance, which was meant as anything but. "Miss Baxter has already agreed to dine with me this evening. I'm sorry to be the bearer of such bad news..." There was challenge in his voice.

Sarah was shocked to see Anita trying desperately to hide her amusement. She looked from one gentleman to the other. What did one do in situations like this?

Eric placed her hand on his arm and pulled her away. Sarah took one step, then stopped when Lord Dean moved before them, halting their progress.

A cold wave stole down her spine. The muscle in Lord Dean's jaw flexed. Eric thrummed with suppressed rage, his arm beneath her hand taut as a bow string. The situation was getting out of hand.

"Correct me if I'm wrong, Earnston, but I do believe Miss Baxter is fully capable of answering for herself." Dean's voice had a resolute edge to its accommodating tone. "Maybe," he continued, "Lady Patricia requires an escort to the supper room instead. She is, after all, who you accompanied to the ball."

Eric had accompanied Lady Patricia?

Sarah glanced at Anita, whose face was rapidly changing to worry as the two bulls refused to give an inch. Lord Kentum, for that matter, stood poised ready to break the gentlemen up should he need to.

Sarah pulled her hand from Eric's arm and stepped away. "I do believe I agreed to have supper with Lady Anita and Lord Kentum, my lords. But you are both most welcome to join us." Lord Kentum smiled and held out his spare arm for her to take. Sarah grabbed it like a lifeline and sighed her relief. "Lord Earnston, Lady Patricia is also most welcome to join us. It will make the supper party all the merrier."

In the small hours of the morning, Sarah stood with the Winters in the foyer, waiting for the ducal carriage to come around. Footsteps sounded from behind, and she turned as Eric strode toward them. Her heart missed a beat when he smiled.

"I'm pleased I caught you before you left, Miss Baxter. I've just learned you'll be one of my guests at Kent in a fortnight."

Sarah nodded. "Yes, I'm looking forward to it. I understand your ancestral home is very beautiful."

"Yes, I certainly think so. I am looking forward to having you there." His fingers entwined with hers hidden beneath her domino.

When his family became distracted, bidding Lord Kentum goodbye, he leaned toward her ear, his breath a light tickling against her skin. "Sarah," he said, causing her to quiver, her body yearning for him. "I will not pressure you, but please, think about my proposal. If your concern stems from the fact we have not known each other long, let me use your time at my estate to become better acquainted, and, maybe by the end of the Season, you may give me your reply."

The sweet expression on his handsome face nearly broke her heart, knowing as she did that she would break his within a matter of weeks. How did you tell a man of this era you would sleep with him, but marriage was certainly not a possibility? She was being cruel, leading him on. Who was she kidding? She felt the connection between them, too. It was like riding an out-of-control freight train that would eventually crash.

And Eric would hate her if he ever found out why she was really here and what she'd done. She cleared her throat, unable to form the lie.

"Allow me to try and win your hand?" Eric asked, his eyes full of hope.

Sarah swallowed the lump in her throat. "You may try, Eric." *But you will fail.*

Eric watched as the carriage disappeared down the graveled drive, and already he missed the woman cosseted inside. He laughed at this new inability to live without a woman.

"Have you asked her yet?"

Eric caught Kentum's eye before looking back to the disappearing coach. "Yes."

"And…what did she say?" Lord Kentum came to stand beside him.

A smile quirked his lips. "She said she would think over it. But, give me time, and I'll win her yet."

"You would want to, and soon. Dean's sniffing around her skirts should make anyone seize the moment."

Eric's eyes narrowed as he remembered Sarah not hours before, drinking and laughing with Anita, Kentum, and that damn Dean.

A few weeks into the season, and he'd fallen for the most beautiful, mature debutante he'd ever met. The thought of the weeks to come on his estate filled his mind. His body roared with the knowledge that he could maneuver her alone and have time with her. "Miss Baxter will be the next Countess of Earnston, Kentum. Do not doubt it."

"What about Lady Patricia?" Kentum asked.

Eric clenched his jaw at a question he himself had been asking. What about Lady Patricia, indeed? Earlier tonight, the chit had actually had the audacity to corner him in an abandoned drawing room and tried to steal a kiss. He had never been so uncomfortable in his entire life. He ground his teeth and met Kentum's gaze.

"I'll have to inform both Lady Patricia and our parents that I've made my choice and it's not one to their liking."

Kentum nodded. "Miss Baxter is a beautiful woman inside and out. You have made a good choice, Earnston."

Eric nodded. "Now all I have to do is convince her of that fact." He sighed.

"Well then"—Kentum clapped him on the shoulder—"may I wish you both happy."

"Thank you. I believe we will be." He watched Kentum enter the ballroom, turned, and ordered his carriage. He scraped his boot against the entrance stairs in the interim.

No longer did nights at gambling dens or places like Mae's at Soho Square hold his attention. For the first time in his life, he wished to spend his nights at home with only one woman sharing his bed.

Sarah...

What he had come to feel for her was an affection so deep and enthralling that time itself would never be able to dim it. He would love her forever.

He was sure of it.

CHAPTER 12

TWO WEEKS LATER, Richard and Sarah arrived at Lord Earnston's estate in Kent early in the morning after spending the previous night at an inn in Aperfield. Anita took her on a quick tour of the home's ground floor, before a maid showed her to her room.

Sarah stopped at the sight of Richard sitting on a chair before the unlit hearth when she opened the door. "What are you doing in here?"

Richard raised his brows. "I asked which room you were given and came to wait for you. We need to talk." He stood and faced her. "What are you doing, Sarah? When are you going to take the device? You cannot tell me you have not had the opportunity to fleece his lordship yet. God knows you've had enough chances; how many more will you need?"

Sarah threw her pelisse onto the bed. "It isn't as easy as that. He has to take off his clothes for me to get it, and for that to occur…" She paused. "Well, you know…"

"You will have to sleep with him." Richard threw his cheroot into the unlit hearth. "I thought you planned on doing that anyway. You like him, and he obviously likes you, so what's the problem? It's not like you're a virgin."

Sarah shushed him and sat down on the opposite chair. "That's not the point. I can't just jump his bones; women of this era don't work that way. He has to court me, woo me." She sighed at Richard's disgusted expression. "I know it sounds lame, but it's actually quite nice to have a gentleman sweep you off your feet."

"And is that what his lordship is doing? Sweeping you off your feet? Because let me tell you, we're leaving the instant we have the device, so don't fall for this rogue. It will only make leaving that much harder."

She rubbed her temples, trying to dispel the oncoming headache. "He's such a nice guy, Richard—you can't help but like him." She shook her head. "His brother was the same, I suspect. He did, after all, try and help me before we fell from the horses. And I had stolen from him."

Richard sat forward. "We know the device is here. Do you want me to secure it? I'm sure at some point he wouldn't have it on him, and I can make my move."

"No, don't do anything," she whispered as two footmen brought in her luggage and left. "I'll get it, I promise. Just give me the month, play along with the celebrations, and don't raise any suspicions."

Richard glared. "One month, and then I'll be taking over, and believe me, I'll do anything to get the device back," he said as he stormed toward the door.

Sarah jumped when he slammed the door shut. A moment later, a young woman bustled into the room.

"Good afternoon, Miss Baxter. I'm Louise, and I've been appointed as your ladies' maid. Lord Earnston was informed you didn't bring yours with you. Is that correct, Miss Baxter?"

"That is correct. Please call me Sarah."

Louise's eyes widened, and she curtsied. "I'm very pleased to meet you, Miss Baxter. Please let me know if there is anything I can do for you."

Sarah sighed at the sight of her luggage piled beside the door. "I suppose I should unpack. You could help me with that."

"No need for you to help, Miss Baxter. I'll have it put away soon enough."

Leaving her to it, Sarah continued to explore the spacious apartment. The teak furniture was light and feminine. A four-poster bed stood against a wall opposite the fireplace, with sensuous-looking, jade-colored silk hanging over the intricately carved canopy. A matching duvet covered the bed. Transfixed, she drank in the room's unexpected opulence and beauty.

A lady's writing desk sat in the corner near the windows, giving any who used it a magnificent, strategically placed view of the garden. Sarah ran her hand over the paper and noted the ink pot already set out. Absently, she picked up the quill and twisted it in her fingers. A half smile lifted her lips at the little details Lord Earnston attended to, to please his guests.

The floors were polished cedar and a lovely, hand-woven rug, soft under foot, ran from the bed to the fire. A comfortable looking settee sat before the hearth, no doubt to curl up onto during a cold winter's day.

The different shades of green in the soft furnishings and window-dressings contrasted with the lighter colored furniture. These in turn highlighted to perfection the different textiles and materials throughout the room. The effect was quite breathtaking. From what she'd seen of the house so far, it oozed class, history, pride, and money. Lots of money.

"This room is beautiful. Don't you agree, Louise?" Sarah asked, sitting on her bed.

"It used to be his lordship's before he became the earl." Louise hung a pelisse in the armoire.

"Really?" Sarah shut her eyes as a twinge of ever-present guilt pricked her. It would have still been his lordship's room had she not caused his brother's death. Of course any trace of femininity would be missing should Eric still sleep here. She could imagine him quite comfortable in the space.

Sarah jumped off the bed to gaze out the windows overlooking the garden and private courtyard below—a walled oasis hedged by strategically placed plants to create patterned beds.

Further away, she could see manicured lawns and wild deer grazing on the meadow. It was a very pretty aspect, especially at this time of year when the flowers were still blooming. Different shades of roses and lavender grew in profusion, the warm day releasing the wonderful aroma to drift into her room.

A knock sounded at the door, and Louise opened it. "A missive for Miss Baxter," a footman said, handing the note to Louise.

Sarah took the letter and opened it. "Louise, would you help me change? Lord Earnston has invited me to ride with him."

"Of course, Miss Baxter."

She quickly changed into her riding gear and left the room to head along the first floor passage.

"Sarah." She turned and smiled as Eric strode toward her. "I'm happy to see you. I hope your travels were not arduous."

"Not at all, my lord. I'm just heading for the stable for our ride."

"Ahh, yes, I look forward to it, but before we go, would you like a tour of some of the house?"

She nodded. "I would love that. From what I've seen already, it's very beautiful." Eric took her arm, and a sense of awareness ran down her spine.

"Well then, let us start with the portrait gallery."

She welcomed having him so close to her again. He walked them toward the south wing, which housed the Grand Gallery, and rattled off names of previous earls, their wives, their children and so forth, the multitude of names soon lost on Sarah.

One painting in particular caught her eye, and she stopped. "Eric, wait, is this you in the portrait?"

He sighed, and a flash of distaste crossed his features. He came to stand before the painting and glowered. "Yes, it's the latest in the collection, painted three years ago by John Jackson."

Sarah fought not to boggle at the name of the artist. How amazing to be painted by such a famous historical artist and yet not know it.

She took in the work. Eric had been painted leaning against an old oak, two wolfhounds lying at their ease near his feet. He seemed thoroughly bored and not the least amused. She smiled.

Eric stilled beside her. "Why do I sense you're laughing at me?" He inspected it again. "It is not as bad as I thought."

"No, on the contrary, I like it very much," she said. "I just think Mr. Jackson has caught the aristocratic side of you more than your true self, that's all."

"I didn't know I had two sides. Very interesting notion, my dear. Would you care to explain your findings?"

Did she? "Well…it's just sometimes you can be so serious, and—forgive me if you take offense at this—cold toward people when in society. For instance," she continued, "the first night we met, you kicked Richard and me out of your home. You didn't even bother to find out why we were there or how we came to be. And in this image, you seem very stately and grand, and he's caught that."

"I would not send you packing now, Miss Baxter."

Sarah laughed. "I wouldn't let you."

Eric gave her a heart-stopping grin and took her arm before continuing with the tour. "You do realize, my dear, that you're not supposed to speak in such a forward manner to a gentleman, do you not?"

"I know," she said, laughing.

They moved on into the grand ballroom, which ran directly behind the gallery, consuming one-half of the first floor space. Sarah momentarily lost her breath. The room was glorious. Its size was scarcely comprehendible; gold gilding wrapped around candle sconces, mirrors, and chandeliers. The room was fit for royalty; she could only imagine how grand it would become in a couple of weeks for Anita's engagement ball.

Large Corinthian columns with carved alcoves housed statues in different poses and scenes. Two fireplaces stood proud and tall at opposite ends of the room. Made from gray granite, they were features in themselves.

Sarah sighed, spellbound. "I have never seen anything so stunning. This room takes my breath away." She stepped further into the area, turning full circle so as to not miss any of it.

"My grandfather replicated the ballroom of Hepsley House in Somerset. Hepsley is owned by an old family friend, and my grandparents first met at a ball under Hepsley's grand roof. My grandfather, loving my grandmother as he did, copied the design and layout to remember that night each and every time they used this room. Everything you see here, you would see at Hepsley. It's quite odd when you're standing in another ballroom many miles away knowing it could well be your own."

"Your grandparents were a love match."

"Their marriage was arranged, but love blossomed between them quite quickly, or so grandmother says at least. And I believe they were very happy together until he died."

"When did he pass?" Knowing she was bound to meet some of Eric's extended family, the last thing she wanted was to offend anyone.

"It would be coming up to twenty-five years now. I was only a young child when he died. He was traveling home from London; the clay soils around here can be quite dangerous in some areas. The carriage slipped and rolled and he was killed. Grandmother never really got over his death."

Sarah frowned as they walked back into the gallery and stopped before a painting of the former Lord Earnston and Eric, painted during their youth. Their eyes *were* the same, and her heart squeezed uncomfortably.

"Don't look so sad, darling. It was a long time ago, and grandmother is quite fine now, I assure you."

She looked up at him, knowing their days were also numbered. Stepping toward him, she leaned up and kissed him. Not for any other reason than she loved him, loved being with him, and would miss him terribly when she left.

"I have to warn you, my dear—if you continue to kiss me in such a way, I will be forced to take drastic measures with you."

Sarah teasingly repeated the gesture. The kiss deepened to a slow, intoxicating embrace. She wrapped her arms about his neck and held on, never wanting to let him go. Never wanting to lose this wonderful gift she'd been given. She pulled back, a little dizzy. "What? Like that, my lord?"

"By God, yes, just like that." Eric pulled her at a clipped speed along the gallery. "Come with me."

She chuckled as they left the south wing, rushing past numerous rooms. The west-facing front held a magnificent view over the deer park beyond. The walls within housed pictures by some of the greatest artists the world had ever seen.

With some trepidation, she realized Eric was a very wealthy and powerful man. What would he do if he ever found out she was common and worked as an archaeologist? She shuddered and pushed the thought aside.

They turned down a main corridor, and she noticed the wing closed off half way along by two large wooden doors. Realizing where Eric was taking her, she pulled him to a stop.

"Eric, I can't go into your room; my reputation would be shot to pieces if anyone saw. What if someone catches us in there? I'll be ruined."

He checked up and down the corridor. By the time she comprehended what he was about to do, he had picked her up and carried her over the threshold of his door.

"Well, it looks like I won that argument," she mumbled.

Eric chuckled and kissed her nose. "Let me show you my chambers, and then I promise we'll go for our ride. Will you if I promise not to molest you in any way, no matter how tempting it may be to do so?"

She threw him a wary glance, not too sure whether to believe him or not. "Okay, but be quick. Being here is making me nervous."

He placed her on her feet, and Sarah shut her mouth with a snap. After seeing the other parts of the home, she had been sure nothing could outdo the grand rooms. She was wrong.

His bed alone was an astounding masterpiece of art, sporting steps on all three sides leading up to the mattress. The headboard, made of dark mahogany, stretched from floor to ceiling. She stepped closer and noted the engraved hunting scene of horses and dogs. The posts were carved to resemble trees with vines climbing up and around their trunks. Silk hangings shrouded the bed and gave privacy when required.

Sarah thought of all the children conceived in this bed. Eric, too, would create his babies there. She bit her lip and turned around on the soft Aubusson rug.

Twin leather chairs, positioned before a marble fireplace, were probably the least extravagant items in the room. She walked around, trailing her fingers along the surfaces of the furniture. An ornate desk with lions' heads at the base of smooth, turned legs stood proudly in one corner. The masculine piece overlooked a picturesque rose garden.

A door on one side of the bed was ajar and, curious, Sarah walked over to peer into Eric's dressing room. "There's another door in there, Eric. Where does that go?"

Watching her from the steps that led up to his bed, he said, "My future wife's dressing room. Beyond that is her bedroom." He paused and met her gaze. "Would you like to see it, Sarah?"

Sarah shut the door, not missing the hidden meaning behind his words. She caught the grin and cocky tilt to his lips and frowned. "Do not think I don't know what you're up to, Eric. And to answer your question, no, I do not need to see that room."

He heaved a disappointed sigh. "Perhaps you would prefer joining me over here?"

She walked straight past him and out the bedroom doors. She was not going to answer that question, either. Her anatomy was already screaming, *Yes! Yes I will join you, thank you for asking*.

No, she would behave herself and head for safer waters, outside on the back of a horse instead of thinking of something else between her legs she'd prefer a lot more.

CHAPTER 13

WITHIN MINUTES, they were outside. The day was warm, the sky a turquoise blue, randomly spotted with fluffy white clouds. A faint breeze stirred the air around them.

"The stables are this way."

Eric took her hand and walked toward the wooden and stone buildings. He left her in the courtyard, and she heard him talk to the stable hands before two horses were led from the stalls.

She watched him saddle her mount and tighten the horse's girth, his muscles flexing with the action. Her attention fixated on his arms before he bent over and gave her a perfect view of his backside in buckskin breeches.

His top boots were soon dusty, and she hardly recognized the sophisticated gentleman she had met in London. Here at his country estate, he was more relaxed and carefree. More her type.

He walked a horse toward her, and she smiled. "She's beautiful," she said, patting the chestnut mare's nose before the horse nuzzled into her hand.

Eric stroked the horse's neck. "Tessa is a modest

fifteen- point-two hands. She's a steady and safe mount, I promise." He pulled her toward him and cupped his hands together. "Here, let me help you up."

Sarah turned and mounted the horse, securing her leg around the horn, then fixing her skirts.

Eric walked over to his own horse and mounted with ease. She envied him his breeches and wished she could have donned a pair to ride. At least if she fell off, breeches wouldn't go over her head, revealing her undergarments and embarrassing her more.

"Are you ready?" he asked.

"Yes." She peeked over her shoulder and noted no one was following them. She frowned. "Eric, should we not have a groom with us for propriety's sake?"

"No."

"No?"

He stopped and waited for her to pull up alongside him, then ran a finger down her cheek and cupped her chin before leaning over and kissing her. "I want you all to myself."

Sarah ran her hand down his jaw. Oh, he was temptation incarnate. "You should not kiss me where everyone can see."

"I do not care." He sat back and smiled. "I would like to show you Westerham before I take you on a picnic."

Panic lodged in her throat, but she only nodded. She couldn't go back into the very town she'd run to on the night she'd killed his brother. "Perhaps we could leave seeing Westerham for another day?"

He smiled and kicked his horse into a trot. "It will not take long."

They rode across fields and, after some time, small cottages popped up along the road leading into town. Sarah remembered Westerham well, as not a lot had changed since the morning she and Richard had fled to London. Dirt footpaths ran alongside the small businesses, and the few locals she could see hurried about with their chores.

A large man with an apron stood before a food supply store specializing in horse grain with the bonus services of a smithy. Just ahead, Sarah could see the Watermill and Brewery. The town really was lovely even if it did harbor the people who could see her hung.

Men on the streets waved as they passed, and Eric responded to each and every one with their given names.

"I'm surprised you know them all so well. I doubt there are many earls who could say the same," she said, smiling at a passerby. She adjusted her seat and refused to look in the direction of the inn as they passed. "Tell me, how is it the son of an earl is so friendly with the locals?"

"My father was a good man and instilled qualities in me I abide by. One of those is to look after my tenant farmers, their families, and this township. We're all reliant on one another. It would be foolish of me to mistreat or ignore them."

"Do you let the common people hunt on your land?" She prayed his answer was to her liking.

"I do. I know a lot of land owners do not, but I'm not one of them."

She touched his arm, taken by an overwhelming urge to hug the generous man. "That is so very kind of you, Eric. You're a true gentleman."

"Lord Earnston, a word if ye please."

They stopped, and Sarah felt the blood drain from her face. *Oh, God, no.*

"Mr. Adams, how can I be of help?"

The innkeeper waddled over as best he could considering his size, his steps faltering when he noticed her. The man frowned and narrowed his eyes.

Sarah smiled and hoped by doing so she would dispel the suspicion that he had seen her before. The night she'd stumbled into his inn...

"Ah, I wanted to talk to ye about old Joe Dee down the road. He's ill and needs caring for, but his family is not around these parts. He's too proud to ask for ye help, so I thought I'd take it on myself to ask."

Eric nodded. "Write down everything I need to know to organize his transportation to his family. My steward will take care of it." He paused. "Is there something else I can help you with, Mr. Adams?"

Sarah met the man's gaze head on. To do anything else would be a catastrophic mistake.

"Do I know ye, Miss?"

She shook her head. "I don't believe so, sir."

The innkeeper scratched his tousled hair. "I'm sure I've seen ye before." He rubbed his chin. "Where have I seen ye before?"

Eric frowned, and she shrugged. "I'm a guest at his lordship's estate. Perhaps you saw us arrive early this morning."

Mr. Adams nodded then shook his head. "Nope, not that." He smiled. "Doesn't matter, it'll come to me in time. I'm sure of it."

Nodding, she swallowed the bile threatening to choke her.

Shit!

If Mr. Adams did remember who she was, she and Richard would... She shook the thought away. She didn't want to think about what Eric would do to them. Whatever it was, it wouldn't be good.

"Well," Eric said, pulling her away. "Good day to you,

Mr. Adams, and don't forget to send my steward the details of Joe's family when you have them."

"Right ye are, my lord," Mr. Adams said and left.

Sarah took a calming breath and welcomed the old barman's departure. They rode out of the town in silence before Eric turned off the main drive that led toward his estate.

"Apologies for not being present when you arrived. The home farms needed my attention without delay. A storm passed through some days ago and some roofs were damaged. I thought I would be back in time."

She waved his concerns away. "Will it take much to repair the damage?"

He placed the reins over his arm and took off his top hat before running a hand through his hair. Sarah's mouth instantly went dry, and her hands itched to run her fingers through his long locks, to pull him down for a brazen kiss.

"All but one cottage will require repairs, though none are too serious. I've assured the families it will be carried out forthwith."

She squeezed his hand. "You're a kind and good man, Eric. I may not have known your father, but I'm sure he would be proud of you."

He pulled his horse to a stop. "Do you know what I think, Sarah?"

"What?" she asked.

"I think Kent suits you, and your temperament would be agreeable to this life and title as my wife." He smiled and put his hat back on.

She raised her brow. "That is to be decided," she reminded him softly.

He tried to hide the disappointment in his eyes, but not quickly enough to escape her notice.

A short time later, he led her into a meadow, then

turned onto a narrow path that ran through the woods. The path appeared well-used by animals and humans alike. "William and I used to play in these woods. There are some old ruins not far from here where we used to pretend to be knights."

Sarah came abreast of his horse. "You miss him."

He frowned. "I do. He was the best of men."

Not wanting to see the raw emotion on his face, she glanced away and blinked back tears. If only she could tell him she hadn't meant to kill his brother. Let him know everything that transpired that night. Perhaps he could forgive her if she just told the truth.

"I abhor them."

"Who?" Sarah asked.

"The couple who broke into our home searching for this," Eric said, pulling the device out of his pocket. "I swore on William's grave I would make them pay for his death, and I will not rest until I do."

Sarah said nothing. What could she say? No, she couldn't tell Lord Earnston the truth. He was still so angry, he'd likely shoot her dead on the spot and think about his actions after the fact. And yet, she couldn't blame him. She, too, would have wanted revenge, had she found a family member the same way Eric had.

Her stomach cramped, from fear or hunger she wasn't sure. She cast him a quick glance and caught him staring at her.

She shifted in her saddle, uncomfortable with the knowledge he was unknowingly courting the woman responsible for his sorrow. How could she, in all conscience, allow him to fall in love with her? She should just steal the damn mapping device and leave as Richard suggested. She was being cruel and for no reason, except her own selfish desires.

"Is there a river nearby?" she asked to distract him and her guilt. "I think I hear water."

"It's the Darent and it's where we shall picnic today." They walked a few hundred yards before he pulled his horse to a stop. Eric dismounted and came over to help her down. Sarah's insides quivered as his hands fastened about her hips. She beat back the urge to lean down and kiss him, to beg his forgiveness for a tragedy entirely her fault.

Taking in the view, she spied the picnic basket beside a large boulder and shaded by an overhead tree. "It seems the food fairies have already arrived." She smiled, and Eric laughed, placing her hands on his shoulders so he could help her down.

She sucked in an aroused breath when he deliberately slid her down his chest.

"The fare is sure to be mouth-watering and satisfying."

She stepped out of his embrace with a laugh. "You, my lord, are flirting with me."

He threw off his hat and laughed. "I must admit I am. Now, perhaps you could come back over here so I can continue my flirtation while holding you."

Sarah threw him a saucy look. "Maybe later." She waited while Eric tethered their horses to a tree branch. "Tessa is a lovely horse." She patted her mare, then walked over to the basket of food.

"She is the foal to one of my best hunt horses," he said, following her. "Alas, she never quite grew high enough to become a jumper herself, but she has a beautiful temperament."

Truly, Sarah thought, Eric did not have one bad tempered bone in his body. It was quite refreshing considering who his mother was. She masked her quiver of revulsion at the woman and took his arm. "Shall we eat?"

Eric took her hand and kissed it. "Of course."

Taking the basket with them, they walked into the meadow and sat beneath an oak tree not far from the crystal clear river. The water flowed over rocks, creating little waterfalls near the shore. When Eric smiled and her heart thumped hard. What was he doing to her? She pulled out two glasses from the basket wanting a drink to calm her nerves.

"They've forgotten the champagne," she said, as Eric headed toward the river. He bent down beside the riverbank, the muscles in his arms bunching as he pulled on a rope. Her gaze hungrily devoured him. Was he teasing her on purpose?

"Here it is." Looking pleased with himself, he held up a bottle of champagne.

She set the glasses on the blanket. "I was wondering what was supposed to go in these."

Eric poured the bubbling liquid into each glass and sat down, loosening his cravat and pulling off his jacket as he did so. This close, Sarah could make out the broad, muscular form beneath his shirt. A light dusting of hair peeked from his opened top and it took all of her self-discipline not to push him down upon the cool grass and…

She grabbed a serviette and fanned her face, the day suddenly too warm.

He searched through the picnic basket and handed Sarah a plate. She smiled her thanks then helped him dish up a meal that allowed them each to sample at least one of each delicacy.

They ate in silence, and Sarah drank in every aspect of his magnificent estate. How lucky to have been born and raised in such an idyllic location.

Eric sat with knees bent and one arm lying lazily over his knee. She laughed when he kicked off his high-boots and flexed his stocking-covered feet. He threw her a cocky grin, and she couldn't wipe away her own smile. Never had she thought an earl could be so…enchanting.

Enticing. Loving.

Finishing her meal, she placed her plate back in the basket. Eric sighed and laid down, shutting his eyes. He looked so comfortable, she impulsively shifted the basket out of the way and laid down as well.

He opened one eye and wrapped an arm around her shoulders, pulling her close. "Are you trying to seduce me, Miss Baxter?"

She snorted and pointed at his feet. "I'm not the one stripping my clothes off." She grinned. "Thank you for today. I'm already having a wonderful time." She wrapped her arm about his chest. "It's so beautiful here, one would wish never to leave, I think."

He kissed her forehead. "I agree."

Then he rolled to his side and Sarah found herself lying on her back staring up at him.

Her breathing increased as he slid a finger down her nose and across her lips. "What are you doing?" she asked, kissing the digit.

"Trying to seduce you." He grinned. "Is it working?" She met his gaze, unable to break the contact. His blue eyes were deep enough to drown in. He was a warm, masculine, wonderful man—everything she could wish for, were she allowed to. Not a breath of wind or sound of an animal scurrying broke the magic that hummed between them.

The stillness was broken when pained expression crossed Eric's face, and he took a deep breath. "There is something I need to tell you, Sarah."

She pushed a lock of hair from his face. "Is it bad?" When he didn't speak, unease skittered across her skin. What was wrong with him?

He ran a hand over his mouth and jaw, then nodded. "I've never done this before."

She pushed him off to sit up and face him. "Never done what?"

He smiled and met her gaze. "Told a woman I loved her." Sarah shut her mouth with a snap, trying to control the half thrill, half panic racing through her.

"And are you now?"

"I am." He pulled her onto his lap. "I'm utterly, devotedly in love with you. I want you to marry me." He gave her a little shake. "Marry me, Sarah."

She shifted and straddled his legs. Her heart ached at her inability to own what she felt herself. Dealing with her abandonment would be bad enough for Eric when she left, without piling on declarations of love, too. At the end of the season, he would hate her. Would think her a murdering tease who ruined families for the enjoyment of it.

"You said you would give me time, Eric." She felt him tense beneath her, and he frowned.

"Are you playing me?"

"No." She near choked on the lie. Biting her lip, she wondered what she could say to make the situation better. But there was nothing to say. Their relationship had been doomed from the beginning.

With no other option available, Sarah leaned forward and brushed her lips against his. She could not say how amusing she found him, how wonderful to be around. How much she loved him. But she could show him.

She met his lips again, and he kissed her back, pulling her into his embrace. She wrapped her arms about his shoulders and allowed desire's firestorm to ignite. His hands held her hips, and he rocked her into his heat, spiraling desire through her blood.

He broke the kiss and suckled her neck, kissing his way down her shoulder. Wanting to feel him, allow him to taste and kiss wherever he chose, she cursed her restrictive riding gown.

Growling, Eric rolled them over, and she found herself pinned beneath him on the ground. She whimpered as his hand cupped her breast. His finger and thumb found her sensitive peak and rolled the bud between his fingers. She shut her eyes and reveled in the touch. His lips teased her flesh at the opening of her gown, and she arched into them, her need so strong it hurt.

Eric's hot and hard desire for her pressed into her thigh, and Sarah wiggled against his member. Her body yearned for him to take her. If he asked, she'd allow him her soul. She lifted her leg around his hip, and their heat joined where it ached most. Eric's deep, throaty moan incinerated any concerns she had about sleeping with him. Birth control, safe sex, and the repercussions of such actions were forgotten as both went past the point of no return.

Cupping her bottom, he squeezed her flesh before lowering her pantalets. She closed her eyes, savoring the feel of his large hands before the cooling grass tickled her skin.

Demanding, conquering, Eric kissed her—and Sarah swept her hand down between them and touched him…

He sucked in a startled gasp and pushed into her hand. Sarah untied his front falls and stroked the silky skin.

"Sarah, I won't take you on the ground. You deserve better."

She opened her eyes and met his gaze, pulling him down for a reassuring kiss. "You will, because if you don't, I think I'll die."

He laughed. "In all seriousness, I cannot take you

here." She rolled her hips and smiled at his pained expression.

"Please, Eric. Don't be cruel."

He growled and sat up. Clutching his coat, he shoved it beneath her bottom. Sarah bit her lip as his gaze froze on her apex. She supposed she might look a little different down there than he was used to. He frowned.

Sarah laughed. "It's the latest fashion in Europe, Eric." He came over her and positioned himself at her core. "I like it," he said.

Burning for him to fill her, she lifted and wrapped her feet about his thighs.

With one thrust, he did.

CHAPTER 14

MINE.

The word chanted over and over in Eric's mind. A mind now hazy with need, desire, and love. All of it mixed around to create a new and intoxicatingly addictive existence.

Feeling light and heat blaze through him, he thrust deep, knowing that sex had never before been so consuming or satisfying. He rocked into her, clasping her arse to heighten the feeling. A voice cautioned him to be gentle, take her slowly, yet he could not. She met his every stroke with one of her own and broke his control.

He wanted to please her, make her first experience with a man something she would never forget for the rest of her life. A life he was going to share with her. Days and nights stretched endlessly before him, filled with lovemaking, marriage…children.

He gentled his touch and kissed her. Showed her how much he adored her. With the chemistry they shared, how could she not agree to marry him? With every gentle touch and kiss, her love became a beacon of light he desperately wanted to reach.

She loved him.

Eric growled when her hands clasped his backside and pulled him into her—a fast learner, his future wife. Her husky moan joined his and, in an instant, his restraint vanished. He wanted to hear that sound again. Wanted her to enjoy him as much as he enjoyed her.

"Eric…"

He quickened his pace and gave her what she wanted. What he wanted. It was madness. Family and staff often used this meadow for outings; they could be caught at any moment. But he could not stop. For weeks, the desire to have her had burned in his soul. For weeks he'd fantasized about her. Wondering what it would be like to seal his fate with her.

And now he had, and he would never rue his choice. "I love you," he whispered against her ear and nibbled her lobe.

She clutched at his back, her nails scoring his skin through his shirt. "Eric, don't stop."

He didn't. Instead, he pushed her until she writhed beneath him and her inner tremors pulsed around him. He wanted her to scream, call out his name, and declare she was his and only his.

She came and never had he won a sweeter victory. Her delicious response pulled him into his own release, and he allowed himself to topple into the void of completeness.

He would freefall forever.

❦

EXHAUSTED, CONFUSED, REPLETE, SARAH STARED AT THE knobby branches of the tree above. She'd never had sex like that. She inwardly cringed at the word *sex*. It had been anything but something as unpoetic as *sex*. They'd worshipped each other, showed without words what they felt for one another.

Love.

She chuckled and drew a deep breath as he rolled off her and lay with his eyes closed, breathing rapidly. She touched his chest and came to lie across it. "You look thoroughly kissed, my lord."

He stroked her hair. "You appear thoroughly ruined, Miss Baxter."

She smiled. "That was wonderful. When can we do it again?"

He grinned impishly. "Not today. I fear if I touch you again, you'll certainly not look fit to be seen."

"You are a little disheveled yourself." She kissed his jaw, his neck, and then his chest, the fine hairs poking out the top of his shirt tickling her lips.

"Sarah…"

"Hmmm?"

"Behave," he growled.

She puffed out an annoyed breath. "Well, you can't blame a girl for trying."

He chuckled and kissed her. The sweet embrace fired their hunger once more. "Damn your appearance. Come here."

Sarah laughed and tried to pull away. "No, you're right. We'd better not. The day is getting on, and you have guests arriving."

"I don't care. It is much better fun here, alone."

"I know it is, but we've already been gone for some time. I would hate to be caught in such a scandalous way." She pushed a lock of Eric's hair from his brow and marveled at his handsome features. "Truly, Eric, we should leave."

With a resigned sigh, he gazed up at the sky and nodded. "Very well." He pulled her to her feet, and Sarah refused the little voice telling her to throw him onto the ground and have her way with him again, to hell with wrong and right.

Instead, she righted her riding gown and spun her hair back into the few pins she could find. She searched about for her undergarments and hastily slid them on. Eric observed her, his eyes hungry and intense, and Sarah fought not to blush.

"Ready?" He kissed her one last time before they packed away the picnic. He left the basket back beside the rock and gathered the horses before helping her to mount.

They rode through open fields, among low sweeping hills. Sarah could see the River Darent winding north through the valley before her, slowly making its way toward the Thames and eventually out to sea.

"How long has your family had the earldom?" she asked, even though she already knew the answer. She had to hear the sound of his voice.

"Since Queen Elizabeth's reign. Not all that long I suppose, in terms of history, but we have been lucky enough to pass the title down through the family from father to son, never having to use any other branch of our lineage."

"So I imagine your family is quite keen to see you settled, wanting such a tradition to continue." Sarah glanced over at him and noted the frown before he masked it.

"Of course, but I will be the first earl to choose his own wife."

A knowing twinkle entered his eyes. She looked away,

unable to hold his gaze over his terrible choice in wives. Her. "All previous marriages were arranged due to social stature or fortune. Recently, I have come to realize that I would like an altogether different union."

Sarah refused to react to the statement, instead focusing on the distant chimney tops she assumed belonged to his home. He adored her. Loved her. Wanted to marry her. The all too familiar feeling of guilt assailed her, and she fought not to blurt the truth and let him have at it. Or her, as it were. "That is just as it should be," she said, her voice buoyant despite the pain stabbing her chest. She cleared her throat to remove the lump lodged there. "How large is your property? I gather from your mention of tenant houses that this is a working farm."

"Just over one thousand acres. We farm mostly crops of various kinds, along with deer and sheep. My tenants reside just out of Westerham. I'll take you to the home farms one day." He said it as if they were truly engaged.

A few moments later, he led her toward the eastern side of the property, an aspect she hadn't seen before. From here, she could see how the home nestled in a valley, a haven for the earls of Earnston for hundreds of years. Nothing had prepared her for seeing it in its entirety from this distance, under glorious sunshine and through crystal-clear air. Sarah sucked in an awed breath at the vision before her.

"This vantage point always takes my breath away. Do you like it, Sarah?" he asked.

Like it? She loved it. It was hard to fathom a home so grand could belong to just one man. "It's amazing, Eric."

Pride filled his eyes. "Come, there's more to see."

CHAPTER 15

LATE THAT AFTERNOON, they arrived back at the estate just as a travelling carriage was being unloaded before the front doors. Sarah dismounted, handed her mount to a waiting stable lad, and followed Eric into the home.

"My lord, your grandmother, The Dowager, Lady Earnston has arrived and requested to see you. She is having tea in her private sitting room."

Eric laughed. "She's early." He met Sarah's gaze, and she read the love he held for his grandparent. "We will join her directly," he told the footman.

They walked into the sun-warmed room, which was furnished with light colored upholstered settees and chairs. Eric's grandmother sat before an unlit hearth, fiercely concentrating over the delicate needlework in her hands.

"My grandmother is in residence most of the year. Her trips to Bath are fleeting and only if the weather is congenial. She believes the waters are advantageous to her health and wellbeing," he whispered leading Sarah toward the dowager. "Miss Sarah Baxter, may I present my grandmother, the Dowager Countess, Lady Earnston."

Sarah curtsied and smiled. "I am very happy to meet you, my lady."

His grandmother stood and bustled toward them. "I'm sure the pleasure is all mine, Miss Baxter. Now, come sit and, Eric, my dear, you may go and occupy yourself for a little while. It want to get to know Miss Baxter over some tea and cake."

Eric laughed. "I do have some correspondence waiting for me. I will return shortly, Miss Baxter. And Grandmamma?"

"Yes, dear?" her ladyship asked.

"Please ensure my guest is welcomed properly into the family."

The dowager shooed him from the room. Left with a matron of the ton, Sarah steeled herself for the ordeal.

The dowager hadn't missed the veiled meaning behind Eric's request, and, from the way she regarded her, it was clear she'd noticed the currents running between Sarah and her grandson.

She rang for tea and then seated herself beside Sarah, sighing as she did so.

"Miss Baxter, first and foremost, may I call you Sarah?"

"Of course, my lady." She dared not refuse her ladyship anything.

"Very good. Now tell me, my dear, how did you come to meet my lovely grandson?"

The image of Eric's lifeless brother flashed before her eyes, and she swallowed the bile that rose in her throat. She probably shouldn't start with the very beginning.

"I met his lordship in London through my friendship with Lady Anita."

Her ladyship smiled. "Oh, Anita, such a lovely girl. Now none of this 'my lady' business, please. I have never been high-in-the-instep. You may call me Rose when we're alone."

"Thank you. That is very kind." Sarah relaxed somewhat at the comforting gesture.

"I must say I'm delighted Eric is taking such an interest in you. We have been waiting an age for him to form an attachment."

Sarah coughed. "I'm merely visiting due to Lady Anita's betrothal to Lord Kentum. I'm sure his lordship is simply being polite with showing me around." She hoped the heat she felt on her face wasn't physically there.

The dowager's knowing twinkle said louder than words that she saw through Sarah's patter.

"I know my grandchild, and if I were a gambler, I would lay odds in your favor. I believe he is in love with you. Eric is certainly not the type of gentleman to lead any young woman astray." She paused as the tea tray arrived and was placed before them.

Sarah sat in silence, her mind a whir of conflicting emotions.

Her ladyship poured the tea and offered a cup. "I think Eric will ask for your hand in marriage."

Sarah choked. She put her cup down and tried to pull herself together. Embarrassment swamped her as Eric's grandmother patted her back.

"Oh, my dear, are you all right?"

She nodded, not sure it was quite safe enough to answer the question. Her eyes watered, blurring the room until it resembled a watercolor painting.

"Now I may be old," Lady Rose continued. "But I'm sure if anyone could tell a man in love, it would be the woman receiving the affection. Don't you agree?"

Sarah flushed. "I believe you may be correct, my lady."

Lady Rose clapped her hands. "I always am, my dear,

and I apologize if my forward manner of speaking makes you nervous. When I was your age, I was the same way. But with the passing of time, you learn to say and do whatever you like while there's still time. So let me assure you, Sarah—my grandson would never allow himself to fall into a situation which could be misconstrued later."

She patted Sarah's hand.

"Now tell me, what is your brother's title? If he has one, of course."

Sarah swallowed hard against threatening tears. "He's a baron, my lady." Another lie, another prick of guilt to add to her conscience.

Her ladyship smiled. "Well there, you see, if your social situation was worrying you, it should not. I myself am a baron's daughter. No lofty titles whatsoever in my family, either, and I still married an earl." Her countenance clouded in some blissful remembrance. "A wonderful man, strong of character and heart, and his grandson is just like him."

Sarah sat back and sipped the lukewarm tea. She thought of Eric's proposal, of how she would love to say yes. It was such a hopeless situation and yet their attraction to one another was impossible to ignore.

The door opened and Sarah smiled, relieved, when Anita walked into the room.

"There you are, Sarah. I have been searching for you everywhere." Anita came forward, and her step faltered when she noted her grandparent's presence. "Grandmother, I didn't know you had arrived. Welcome home." She gave her grandmother a kiss and plopped onto a nearby settee.

"I only arrived today, darling. I was just having a cozy tête-à-tête with Miss Baxter." Her ladyship smiled at Sarah.

Anita poured herself a cup of tea and sat back.

"Well, my dear, are you going to tell us what entertainments you have planned?" Her ladyship asked.

"Tomorrow we're going out in the carriages to pick strawberries." Anita turned to Sarah. "Strawberries are Lord Kentum's favorite fruit. And since he has to go away tomorrow for a day or two, I thought I'd surprise him with a treat when he returned."

Sarah smiled, inwardly amused such a simple outing could cause such excitement. How things had changed. The closest to strawberry picking Sarah had ever come was deciding which punnet to buy in the supermarket.

"It sounds like a wonderful idea," she said.

"What is a wonderful idea?" Eric asked, entering. He stood behind Sarah, and a prickling of awareness ran through her.

"We're going strawberry picking tomorrow, Eric. Can you send word to the stables and make sure everything is ready after breakfast? I think it best we leave before it gets too warm." Anita took one last sip of her tea and stood. "Well, I must dash. Lady Patricia has picked out the most ghastly music for my betrothal ball, and I'm afraid I must say no."

Sarah watched her leave. So, Anita, the Dowager Lady Earnston, and Eric all thought her the perfect woman for him. Had she not entered his life under such heinous circumstances and with criminal intent, she would be entitled to think the same.

But she could not.

When she was sure no one was taking heed of her whereabouts, Sarah stepped out onto the terrace. Dinner had gone well, if one could describe success as dodging barbs from Eric's mother.

Breathing in the fragrant night air, she walked along the flagstone patio. The gardens were dark and mysterious while the house shone like a pillar of light.

At the sound of whispered voices, she slowed her steps. She peeked around an ivy clad window and saw Lady Earnston and Lady Meyers, Patricia's mother, in the library.

Leaning closer to hear what they were saying—Sarah froze, shocked by what she heard.

"Did you see her in London dancing attendance on Lord Dean, Lady Meyers? The little Baxter minx probably doesn't know she will have to wait a few years before she can wear the ducal diamonds, since the boy's grandfather is still alive. It makes me serenely pleased she may be our age before coming into the title."

Sarah reeled at the venomous tone. She knew Eric's mother disliked her and saw her as a threat to Lady Patricia, but such abhorrence?

"Obviously a mere earl isn't good enough for that social climbing trollop. Not," Lady Earnston said, whispering, "that I mind. I would refuse to accept her as the future Countess of Earnston in any case."

Lady Meyers gasped in horror, as if nothing could be worse in the world. "Did you see how she threw herself at Eric at the Cottlestones' ball? She practically stroked him on the ballroom floor. It's any wonder your dear boy was mesmerized. He probably couldn't walk when he finished the dance."

Lady Earnston muttered angrily, her outrage clear, and then her eyes narrowed. "Well, I'm relieved to see he seems to be over his bout of desire for the woman," she replied. "He's quite smitten by Patricia, if dinner is anything to go by. I believe this little fixation on Miss Baxter is finished. I'm sure he only invited her down here because Anita has befriended her. Trust me when I say it will be only weeks before we're placing a betrothal announcement in the papers."

"I do hope so," Lady Meyers eagerly replied.

Anger coiled in Sarah's gut. How dare they speak about her in such a way? She had done nothing but act a lady since entering their world. Granted, she had allowed Eric privileges, but they did not know that. And as for Eric bestowing favor toward Lady Patricia—what a load of bull. He had asked after her day at dinner. Last time Sarah checked such a question did not lead to marriage or insinuate undying love.

She stormed back toward the downstairs parlor, then stopped. What was she doing? She couldn't go inside and give the high and mighty countess a public set down. And what was the point if she did? She was playing Eric. Using him to secure the device.

Wasn't she?

Pain tore through her breast, causing her to crumble onto a stone bench. Who was she kidding, other than herself? For a few weeks now, she had experienced a strange blossoming in her heart—a feeling she'd never had before.

Eric had long ago stopped being a means to an end. He was the reason she eagerly attended every ball, the reason she got out of bed each morning, and the reason she no longer wanted to leave this time.

She cursed at her weakness and silently apologized to Richard. Truthfully, she could have stolen the device on a number of occasions. But she had not. For the simple reason she didn't want to leave him.

She loved him.

She swiped at her eyes. What a pickle she'd made of things. Again.

❦

"ARE YOU ALL RIGHT, SARAH? I SAW YOU LEAVE AND WAS worried you'd taken ill." Eric noted her jump at his words. Helping her to stand, he ran a hand over her cheek and marveled at the softness of her skin. The light from the library shone against her profile, showing off the slight blush his touch brought forth.

"I'm very well. Perhaps a little warm, but otherwise fine." She stepped back and out of his reach.

He frowned at her detached tone and allowed her space. "The air is very warm tonight. I should not be surprised we have a storm in a day or two."

She nodded and started to stroll along the terrace. "I went for a walk today and saw you have a lake. I gather since there's a rope hanging from one of the trees that you swim there."

Eric placed her hand on his arm and pulled her close. "We do. In fact, if you're feeling adventurous, we could walk down there right now."

The smile she bestowed on him warmed his blood. "I was born for adventure."

"Come then." He pulled her along the flagstones before helping her down the steps. "I suppose I should ask if you can swim, although if you're drowning I can always rescue you."

Sarah laughed. "I can swim very well, no need to act the hero." She ran a little to keep up with his strides. "Are you going to allow us to swim? It's nearly the middle of the night."

The thought of her shift, soaking wet and clinging to

her delectable form made his steps increase. "I'm willing if you are." They came to a stop on the grassy verge of the lake.

"Are you daring me?"

Eric shuffled out of his coat and started to untie his cravat. "If I dare you, will you take off your gown?"

"Maybe."

"Well then I dare you." Eric watched, enthralled as Sarah walked toward him, her hips swaying in silent seduction in the moonlight.

"Will you unbutton me? I have no maid."

The grin on her lips said without words that she was teasing him. He tamped down the desire that shot to his nether regions as he turned her about and started to do as she asked. "I hope there is a shift under this gown. Swimming is one thing, but to swim naked could prove too trying for my heart."

"I have a shift on so your health is assured."

He highly doubted that. Eric made quick work of her fastenings and stripped himself down to his knee- high breeches. He helped Sarah wade into the water and welcomed the cooling change of temperature. There was no breeze, and the air was thick with moisture and fragrances.

They swam to the centre of the lake and Eric found the rock that protruded and allowed swimmers to stand above water. Sarah joined him, only the thin layer of her underwear keeping them apart. His gut clenched at the sight of her breasts, wet and bathed in silver moonlight. She looked like an angel he wanted to keep on earth forever.

"This is so refreshing. You should tell your guests they're free to use this swimming hole as much as they please. It's marvelous!" She pushed away from him and floated on her back.

Eric bit back a groan when he noted the shift was unmistakably transparent. "Are you torturing me on purpose?" Sarah laughed, and he knew she was. *Minx!*

"Maybe a slight flirtation, but not torture."

He dived under the water and swam to where she was. Surfacing, he clasped her about the waist and walked her the couple of steps to the wooden jetty. Her slight form fitted against him perfectly, her light shift allowing him to feel every inch of her figure. He hardened and groaned when she wrapped her legs about his hips and teased them both by sliding against him.

"You do torture me," he said, his voice husky with need. She stared at him, her eyelashes sporting tiny droplets of water on their ends.

"You torture me, as well. So I suppose we're even."

Eric kissed the grin from her lips, taking all that he could. It was like she was made for him, fitted him like the finest made Hessian boot. "I want you. All of you."

"You have me." She gasped as he slid his hand down her hip and ground her against his sex. An ache thumped in his groin, and he fought the impulse to take her here and now. He couldn't take her in a lake. First a meadow and now a swimming hole. He was starting to act like a barbarian.

"Do you trust me?" He caught her gaze and held it. "Of course. Always."

Relief poured through him hearing the words aloud.

"Then just enjoy…"

SARAH BIT HER LIP AS ERIC KISSED HER TO WITHIN AN INCH of her sanity. This Regency rake could certainly kiss well. Her body ignited in fire and all she wanted was sex. Hot, hard, fulfilling sex, but the innocent debutante she was portraying had to let Eric mete out what would happen next.

It was hardly helpful for an impatient woman.

His hand skimmed down her stomach, his fingers pulling up and bunching the shift around her waist. Her breathing hitched as his hand delved between her legs and played, rubbed, and fondled her aching core.

It was all she could do not to rip open his frontfalls and make him take her, fulfill both their needs. He kissed beneath her ear, his tongue running up the side of her neck and she shook. "Now who's torturing who?"

His deep, resounding chuckle was all the answer she received before he slid one then two fingers within her. His touch felt so good, made her burn hotter than she ever had before. Each stroke hit the special spot within her, his thumb paying homage to her bud. Sarah wrapped her arms about his neck and rode his hand. She was so close to bliss she could taste the sweetness on her tongue.

"Let go, Sarah. Enjoy me as much as I'm enjoying you."

She cried out in the quiet night as wave after wave of orgasmic convulsions swirled through her core. Her breathing ragged, she fought to gain a semblance of control. A pointless exercise as she'd well and truly lost all her faculties and control. Had done so the moment Eric touched her.

She kissed the damp skin on his shoulder before meeting his gaze. "I'll never forget this night, Eric. Ever."

His lopsided grin made her belly somersault. "Then that would make two of us."

CHAPTER 16

THE ARRAY of carriages was loaded with picnic baskets and blankets. The few family members and select friends already at the estate walked about, eager for the outing to begin.

Sarah spied Eric checking over the conveyances and chatting with his guests. She took in his tight breeches, shirt, and loosely tied cravat and yearned to stroll over and kiss him good morning.

"I'm going to stay behind," Richard said, startling her. He lowered his voice. "It will give me an opportunity if you understand my meaning."

"He carries the device. It won't be in the house," she responded, her voice sharp.

"I'm staying in any case. I've already asked his lordship if I could have the use of his desk in the library, and he agreed."

She bit her lip and frowned. "Don't get caught, whatever you do. And be more careful this time; leave nothing out of place." She waved to Anita who gestured for her to come.

"Don't worry about me." He glanced up at the sky, and Sarah followed his gaze. "I don't know how long you'll be out picking strawberries, but by the look of that storm coming in, it won't be long."

"Perhaps it will go around us. Either way, the carriages all have hoods, so we'll be fine." She moved off the steps and started to walk toward the vehicles, yelling over her shoulder, "I'll see you later, Richard," and walked up to Eric. "Which carriage am I to travel in, my lord?"

Eric smiled down at her and fleetingly touched her hand. "You'll ride with me and Grandmamma, Miss Baxter. Come." He led her to where the dowager already sat in an enclosed coach.

Disappointment that she would miss traveling in the open-roofed vehicles assailed her. "Why are we not traveling in one of those carriages, my lord?" Sarah asked, nodding toward the line behind theirs.

"I thought it best for Grandmamma, but you are more than welcome to travel with Anita if you wish."

As if she'd leave his side, even for her friend. Besides, Lady Earnston had crammed in beside Anita. "No, that's fine. I'll travel with you, my lord," she said coolly.

Eric grinned and helped her into the carriage.

They traveled for nearly an hour before stopping in a field full of strawberry plants, the little red fruit bursting to be picked. Sarah had to admit, as simple as the outing was, it was still immense fun. Until those overcast clouds turned more ominous, and a fat, wet plop of rain landed on her cheek.

They had barely packed up the carriages when lightning flashed and thunder boomed, sending some of the ladies into a fit of panic. Eric took charge of the madness, hurrying everyone into their coaches so the party could head out of the weather.

"We need to leave now," he said to their driver. "The weather is coming from the east, and the small creek we crossed is prone to flooding. If we don't cross it soon, we'll not make it home tonight."

Eric's grandmother appeared pale, and Sarah took her hand. The storm did seem to become more ferocious by the minute, but it was only a rainstorm, after all. On the other hand, it was enough to scare the other women in the group witless.

Eric met her gaze and entered the carriage just as the rain started to come down in torrential form. The coachman hollered to the horses and they were off.

They made good time, considering the weather, but at the first profanity from the driver, Eric jumped out. His curse was audible, and he leaned back into the carriage to take his grandmother's hand.

"Grandmamma, the brook is coming down, and we need to get you home. The water is not too deep at the moment, but we have time for only one more carriage to cross safely. I'm going to transfer you into the front carriage."

"But what of Sarah? I cannot leave her here unchaperoned. What will her brother say?"

Eric cringed. "There is only room enough for one person, Grandmamma." A pained expression crossed his face. "With your health, I cannot allow you to stay."

Sarah nodded. "He's right, my lady. You must go. Tell Richard I'm fine and will be home as soon as the water level drops. I'm sure it won't be too long."

The dowager grumbled. "You know what this will mean, Eric."

He lifted her from the carriage and carried her to the other vehicle. "I know," he said.

Sarah grabbed an umbrella beside her seat and

followed. She gasped at the chilling wind and the swirling river before them. The small tinkling stream they'd crossed this morning was now a fast flowing, murky waterway like the Thames.

"My lord, are you sure it's safe for another carriage? The water looks awfully dangerous."

"I know the levels, Miss Baxter, and when they're not passable. We still have time." Eric called out to the driver and the carriage moved off.

The horses pranced as their hooves touched the chilling water, but stepped in to wade across. The ladies screamed as one horse lost its footing and the carriage shifted sideways a little. Their coachman ran into the river and waded out to the terrified horse. He grasped its reins and helped guide it to the other side. Sarah sighed in relief when the coach climbed the opposite embankment, the ladies soaking wet, but out of harm's way.

"Sarah, I'm sorry."

She shrugged. "It doesn't matter. I'm just glad everyone is safe." They returned to the horses and Eric led them off the road, away from the rising river. He unhitched the team and tied them to a nearby tree before returning to the coach. "Best, I think, not to have them hitched. They could bolt with this lightening around."

Sarah nodded and stepped into the carriage. Eric followed her, his clothing as soaked as hers. "How long do you think we'll be stuck this side of the river?"

Eric shrugged. "These creeks fall as quickly as they rise. I would think by tomorrow morning it will be passable."

The wind howled outside, and the carriage rocked. Sarah shivered and rubbed her bare arms.

"You're cold." He pulled out a carriage blanket and sat beside her.

Sarah welcomed the blanket's warmth when he placed it about her shoulders and rubbed her back.

"Better?" he asked.

She nodded. "Much, thank you. But what about you?"

"I'll be fine," he replied, despite the way his teeth chattered.

Noting his blue lips, she said firmly, "Take off your clothes, Eric. You'll die of pneumonia if you stay in those wet garments."

"I don't believe that would be wise, do you?"

Cursing in a manner most unladylike to the period, she untied his cravat to strip away the soaked clothing. "I'll not have you die of a cold." Fear rose with the thought. People in this time died of such trifling illnesses all the time—and that was not even to mention the possibility that he could die of exposure if he didn't get warm. She stilled her ministrations when his finger wiped a droplet of water from her nose.

"I'm feeling decidedly warm already, Miss Baxter. Pray continue."

Sarah sat back, realizing she was no longer feeling as cold, either. "You're incorrigible."

"A rake's trait."

The urge to kiss him, to succumb to the desperate need blossoming between them was too great to resist. She separated the lapels of his coat and pushed them from his shoulders. She burned to be close to him. To feel his skin against hers. His heat. His heart.

She yanked the cravat from his neck and ripped open his shirt buttons while he untied the back of her gown. He pushed the soaked material from her shoulders, and the chill air kissed her skin.

Sarah broke the kiss and peeked down at the light shift she wore beneath her dress, separating her from complete nakedness. Pulling at the ties, she let the garment gape at her chest, careful not to expose her scarred arm.

Eric's gaze was scorching, his breathing rapid. He slid his hand over her waist to cup her breasts. She bit her lip and prayed for patience.

"You're so beautiful." He pulled her against him and took her lips in a searing embrace. She wondered if it would always be like this between them. As if they could never get enough, be close enough, to one another.

Grasping her hips, he lifted her onto his lap. His hands traveled down the back of her legs, pulling her dress along with them. Sarah wiggled upright as best she could to step out of it altogether.

She watched as Eric ran a hand through his hair. "Are you not going to do the same, my lord?"

In response, he leaned against the squabs and pulled off his breeches. She took a calming breath when he threw his shirt across to the opposite seat. His chiseled chest, the six pack abs leading down to his hard, engorged heat now noticeably jutting against his abdomen made her quake. She licked her lips and straddled his legs, the cool velvet seat soft beneath her knees.

He gasped when she rocked against his rigid flesh. His hands bit into her hips, and she lifted off him before impaling herself on his manhood, causing him to cry out.

He was so warm, so amazing, and so good. The fact she loved him seemed to heighten the experience, make everything more…everything.

He growled and kissed her neck, and Sarah rasped her fingers through his hair.

"I love you, Sarah."

The declaration—the plea—tore at her heart. *I love you, too,* her mind promised, but she remained silent. He laid his head against the squabs, and Sarah kissed his ear.

"Yes," he said, his hands running up her back.

Need roared between them, and their joining became frantic. The carriage rocked and the storm outside, the rising river, fell away, forgotten, as they pushed each other to the brink of bliss.

Eric drove forcefully into her, and she gasped. The delicious slide to orgasm came quickly, and Sarah clutched his shoulders as she leaned back while her release overtook her.

Distantly, she heard herself sigh his name before he, too, fell over the edge and into ecstasy.

After, he drew her close and kissed her. "You're a remarkable woman," he said, pulling the blanket about her shoulders once more.

She sighed and cuddled into his heat. Her heart crumbled into her chest. If only that were true.

CHAPTER 17

Sarah awoke with a start when the carriage jerked forward. She sat up and pulled the blanket about herself before glancing outside.

The day appeared clear, save for a few darkish clouds spotting the sky. Hearing Eric's voice, she froze, then sighed with relief when she realized he was only speaking to the horses.

She set about finding her clothes—squealing with surprise when the carriage door opened.

"Good morning, beautiful."

Sarah rubbed her eyes, fairly sure she made the least beautiful person at that moment. "Good morning," she said, cursing the blush that stole over her cheeks.

"Get dressed, my love, and I'll return you home. The water has receded enough to safely do so."

"Just give me five minutes."

Eric leaned in to kiss her, and she dropped the blanket, allowing him to gather her into him. Her nipples brushed his damp shirt, sending delightful pain to her core.

He growled. "Dress, and quickly, before I debauch you again in the carriage."

She threw him a saucy grin. "I wouldn't complain."

He patted her bottom and set her back on the seat. "My little minx. Dress. I have to try to limit the scandal my actions last night have caused. Although I'm not sure we'll escape unscathed if my mother has her way."

Sarah grabbed her dress as the door closed, trembling when the damp material touched her. At least she wouldn't have to wear it for long once they arrived at the house.

Dressed, she stepped from the carriage and stretched. The damp gown and slight wind sent goose bumps across her skin, and she reached inside to grab the blanket.

Eric stood before the river, silently watching the abating waters. "I'm ready." She walked up to him and slid her hand down his back, needing to touch him whenever she could.

He looked down at her, his face troubled. "Everyone will expect us to marry now that we've spent a night alone. And we have slept together twice now, Sarah. You could be with a child." He caught her hands. "Have you thought about my question at all?"

She nodded. "I know what you're saying, but last night, with the storm and dangerous situation, was unavoidable. Surely they wouldn't expect such a thing. Should you have been stuck here with Lady Patricia, would you be declaring your betrothal today?"

Eric ran a hand through his hair. "The family and my honor would have demanded it, and so, yes, I would."

She stepped back. "Even though you say you love me?"

"I would have no choice, to save her reputation. And I will not have yours ruined, either. You will marry me, Miss Baxter."

Sarah narrowed her eyes. "I will not."

Dropping her hands, Eric stormed to the carriage and climbed up on the box. "Best be getting in, Miss Baxter. We'll discuss this when we're home."

Glaring at his back, she followed his order. Damn the man. And damn the blasted weather. She should have swam across the stupid river and left him here. Sarah flopped onto the squabs and crossed her arms. They would not make her marry a man just because she spent the night with him, or because he made her body burn with every touch. And if they thought they would force her into something against her will, they had another thing coming.

ERIC WAITED FOR SARAH TO CLIMB INTO THE CARRIAGE. What was wrong with her that she didn't want to marry him?

He was wealthy, titled, and in love with her. He was a much sought after bachelor in town, yet she continued to evade his offer for her hand.

Why?

The carriage door slammed, and he took a calming breath. Picking up the reins, he tapped the horses' rumps, and started the short drive to his estate.

Lord Stanley awaited them on the front steps when they entered the gates. Eric steeled himself for the coming confrontation over Sarah's ruined reputation. Well, he had no qualms in marrying the woman; it was the woman herself putting up a fight.

He pulled the carriage to a halt.

"Eric. Sarah. We were all so worried about you." Anita rushed down the stairs and opened the carriage door before the footman could do it. "Come inside—we have baths prepared for you in your rooms." She met Eric's gaze. "The storm was so ferocious we've not slept a wink for worry."

Eric climbed down and helped Sarah alight. He ground his teeth when she pulled away and stepped out unassisted. "Ferocious but fast moving it seems," he drawled, signaling for the groom to take the horses and carriage away.

"Even so, what a frightening experience for you."

Sarah smiled at Anita's concern. "I'm fine, do not worry. I'm just a little tired. May we go in now so I can have that wonderful bath you mentioned?"

Fussing over her, Anita called directions to the staff. Eric saw them into the house and turned to meet her brother's cold stare evenly.

"Lord Earnston, your mother, Lady Earnston, and I request your company in the library when you're refreshed," Lord Stanley said.

Eric nodded. "I'll be down shortly." And there it was. Society's rules and strictures about to crash down onto his and Sarah's shoulders. He ambled to his room and sent word to Sarah to meet him in the library before luncheon.

After he'd bathed, he looked at himself in the mirror and fussed with his cravat. The image of Sarah's naked form, her nimble hands pulling it from his neck, assailed him. His soul roared with need and possession.

Marshaling his desires, he went downstairs. Raised voices came from the library, and he quickened his steps toward them.

His mother paced the floor, her face a picture of disgust. His grandmamma, on the other hand, remained seated, seemingly more relaxed than one ought in such a situation. Richard and Sarah merely sat on settees, their sober expressions giving little away.

"What is going on here?" Eric asked.

"What, indeed." His mother came over and poked him in the chest. "How could you, Eric? How could you keep Miss Baxter out all night when you're all but betrothed to Lady Patricia?"

Eric fought to keep his temper in check. He met Sarah's less than amused glance and silently sent her his strength. "There was never an understanding between myself and Lady Patricia, as you well know, Mother. And as for keeping Miss Baxter for an evening, it was either that or risk her life. She is home now and no harm done." Eric didn't miss Lord Stanley's raised brow at his declaration.

"You must marry, and that is all there is to it," his grandmother declared cheerfully, picking up her needlework.

"Out of the question," Sarah said. "I will not be forced into marriage solely because I was caught in the rain with a gentleman."

"I heartily agree with Miss Baxter," his mother said, nodding.

Eric inwardly groaned. "Miss Baxter, think of your reputation." Her jaw set in a stubborn line, and he looked to her brother for support. Why wasn't the man saying anything?

"I have spoken to our guests, Eric, and under the circumstances they have agreed to keep Miss Baxter's name safe from any scandal. There is no reason for you to marry, unless something happened last night." His mother raised her eyebrows in question.

Eric swallowed.

"Nothing happened," Sarah said. "We were soaked through and sat in the carriage the whole night freezing. First light, Lord Earnston hitched the horses and brought us home. End of story. Now if you'll excuse me, I'm going for a walk."

His mother grabbed her arm. "Not so fast, Miss Baxter. I knew there was a reason I did not like you from the moment we met, and I think it's about time I explain my reasons why."

"Don't you ever speak to Miss Baxter like that again, Mother." Anger pumped through Eric's veins at his parent's rudeness. "I apologize on behalf of her ladyship."

"Let her speak. She obviously has something to say." Sarah sat back down, her expression unreadable.

"I never wished to hurt you, Eric, but I have come across some very interesting information that I asked my lawyer to delve into. In fact," she paused, "I wonder why any of us didn't do this sooner. But then, people usually take what others say as truth."

Sarah lifted her chin though her face paled. "And what truth is that, my lady?"

His mother smirked and motioned toward a letter she held in her hand. "I'm just curious if you've ever heard of a book called *Debrett's*, Miss Baxter?"

Sarah nodded. "I have."

"I should have investigated your brother the moment I met you. Why, he's not even a baron is he, and never will be. In fact, there is no record of your family in England at all, and I can prove it."

"What are you talking about, Mother? Miss Baxter?" Eric caught the worried exchange between brother and sister. "What is this all about?"

"Yes, Miss Baxter. Please do us all a favor and explain who you are?" his mother asked triumphantly.

A cold knot of fear curled in his gut. "Miss Baxter, if you would come with me." He pulled her from her chair and led her from the room. A moment later, he ushered her into his library and closed the door.

She walked toward his desk and sat in a chair opposite

his. Taking a seat, Eric regarded her over the four feet of mahogany and noted the woman he'd come to adore appeared guarded. But why?

"Is your name Sarah Baxter?"

"Yes."

He sighed and leaned back in his chair. "Then what is my mother talking about?"

"I don't deserve you or your love."

He stood and came around the desk to pull her into his arms. "Why would you say such a thing? You do deserve to be loved and by me. It is my choice."

"You don't understand."

She tried to pull free, but he tightened his hold, keeping her close. Where she belonged. "Then explain it to me so I do understand."

"I cannot marry you, Eric. Ever?"

Sarah bit her lip, a small frown line forming between her brows. "I need to be honest with you, and I haven't been. I've been lying to you, and your family, and I cannot do it anymore."

"Well then, for God's sake, hurry up and tell me what is going on."

🎔

"You have something we want." At his befuddled and increasingly frustrated expression, Sarah knew she could only rip off the truth like a bandage from a wound —quickly.

"The peculiar your brother treasured is mine."

For a moment, disbelief colored his features, followed closely by denial, then anguish… "What?"

Sara repeated her admission, and he paled. The urge to

clutch at him, apologize profusely, and beg forgiveness warred within her, but she could not. He deserved better than what she'd given him. Realization dawned on his face and, like a knife severing her in two, she knew they were over.

"Please, do explain what that means exactly."

The cold timbre of his voice made her quake. Sarah ignored the fear making her want to flee and sat back down. "I think you know what that means."

Rage, brutal and murderous, washed over his features. He ran a hand through his hair and swore. The love she'd seen in his eyes only this morning was replaced by a cold mask that chilled her core.

"And you were willing to commit murder and sell yourself like a whore to get it back?"

Voice as steady as she could make it, Sarah said, "If I told you the truth, you wouldn't believe me. You need to return it to me, my lord, and leave it at that."

"Answer the damn question." His voice was deadly.

"I cannot."

Eric towered over her, his face close to hers as he gripped her arms, only a squeeze away from painful. "You will if you want to live, Miss Baxter."

She cringed, and the truth tumbled out, the words falling over each other. "I'm an archaeologist by trade. We were excavating an area near Westerham, and I left an electronic mapping device behind. It was a silly mistake. From what our reports told us, your brother had found it. I returned to take it back and made an even bigger mess of things. My father demanded I try again, and so you see, here I am."

"Yes, here you are," he said, his voice devoid of warmth. "What sort of idiot do you think I am, Miss Baxter? Archaeologist? There are no women archaeologists, and certainly not ones digging about with strange peculiars like this." He gestured to his pocket.

"Not from your time, perhaps." Sarah focused on his desk, anywhere but his vacant eyes.

"Excuse me?"

It was too late to save herself now. "Your mother was right. Lord Stanley is not my brother. He is my father's head archaeologist. My family owns a company called TimeArch, and we specialize in archeological time travel digs."

Eric didn't try to hide his disbelief.

"We own a company just outside of London, near Reading."

He frowned. "There is no business named TimeArch in Berkshire."

"Not in this time, my lord, no."

Taking a deep breath, he pinned her with his gaze, demanding she tell him everything. "And you expect me to believe this fanciful tale?"

"Did you never wonder how I just appeared in society? Almost like magic and out of thin air." Sarah made an inadequate gesture. "Your mother can find no mention of our births here in England or abroad. Why do you think that is?"

Eric glared at her. "Because you, madam, are a very fine actress."

She shook her head. "No actress, just not from your time." She turned and walked toward the windows overlooking the magnificent gardens. She took only two steps before his commanding voice rolled over her.

"What does the device do?"

She held out her hand, signaling for the object. Shockingly, he drew it from his coat and slapped it into her palm. Amazed, he stared as she flicked a hidden latch to open it, revealing a multitude of button-like objects. She swiped her finger across the screen and the device lit up like a candle before a voice sounded from inside asking for coordinates. Eric snatched it back, only to toss it to the floor.

"How does it work?" he asked.

Sarah picked it up and typed in her passcode. She handed it back and, grudgingly, he took it. "If you read the screen, it's probably saying that no satellite signal can be found. Which, of course, is right, as in 1818 there are no satellites in space. But the device would normally locate you, wherever you were in the world, and map any area you wish."

"You played me, used me to your own ends." He threw the device back to her. "Well, you've got what you wanted now, and a good tumble while you were here. Take the damn thing. I never want to see it or you again."

Shame and disgust at her actions made her hands tremble. "I did intend to use you at the beginning to gain access to the device, but it certainly is not how it ended. I couldn't care less about the device now. I only care about you."

Scoffing, he stepped back behind his desk. "How many men have you fucked to get your way, Miss Baxter?" He laughed, the sound chilling Sarah's blood. "You were never a virgin, were you? I should have known… You were very apt in your lovemaking."

She swiped at a tear. His disgust left her feeling hollow and ashamed. How he must hate her to say such things.

"How many men have you slept with, madam?"

She swallowed. "Eric…"

"Answer me now, God damn it." He rubbed his chest and pinned her with his gaze. "Are you sleeping with Lord Stanley or whoever he is?"

"No."

He fisted his hands and tried several times to speak before the words finally came out, hard as a slap. "The innkeeper. That's why he recognized you. You *were* the one." Quickly, he strode over, grabbed the sleeve of her dress, and ripped it off. He reeled back at the sight of the scar that marked her arm. "The sight of you and what we've done together sickens me."

"I'm sorry. I never meant—"

"Oh, I'm sure you didn't mean to ruin our lives, but you did." He shook his head, the muscle in his jaw flexing. "You only had to ask for the device, and my brother would've given it to you. Instead, you took a different path, and a young man in his prime lies rotting in the ground."

Sarah swallowed the lump wedged in her throat at the truth of his words.

"I will not speak of your admission to my family as the distress would be too great. Should they learn I harbored the very woman who'd caused their suffering, it would be too cruel. You will attend the betrothal ball tonight as if nothing has happened, other than the disagreement with my mother. You have until tomorrow morn to get off my land, or I'll throw the full force of the law at your pretty head. Now, get out. I never want to see you again."

CHAPTER 18

SARAH SPENT the remainder of the afternoon in her room. Anita consoled her as best she could, but it was of no use. She felt as though her heart no longer beat now that Eric was lost to her.

Their argument and the awful things he'd said played over in her mind, tormenting her and tripling her guilt. Thoughts of his brother's final moments haunted her whenever she closed her eyes.

"You'll have to attend the ball, Sarah. You must, for your own reputation, put on a brave face."

Sarah wiped the endless tears from her eyes and nodded. "I know. Although I'm more than certain Eric will loathe my presence."

"He loves you. I'm sure in time he'll forgive whatever has torn you apart today, and you will reconcile—"

"There is no future for us." Sarah stood and rang for her maid. Already, the day was giving way to the night, and she had a ball to prepare for, no matter how much she didn't wish to go. What did it matter if Eric threw her and Richard out in front of his guests? They were leaving for the capital tomorrow anyway. As soon as they made their London home and the device that would send them catapulting two-hundred years into the future, nineteenth century England would cease to exist.

The thought depressed her more than she ever thought it would.

THE BALL BEGAN, AND THE CONVERSATION ABOUNDED WITH flattery and admiration over the multitude of decorations and the magnificent room. Sarah listened to it all with a detached air, feeling like an outcast. A fallen woman the ton waited to devour. The music washed over her like a death knell, and she stood out of the way like a seasoned wallflower, wondering when she could make her departure.

Time passed in a haze of despair. She grabbed a glass of champagne from a passing footman, needing the fortitude supplied by the alcohol.

A short while later, she watched with growing trepidation as Lady Patricia caught sight of her and strolled her way. "Miss Baxter, I cannot say that your departure tomorrow is unwelcome. I so look forward to the time when your face will be nothing but an unpleasant memory."

Sarah swallowed, fighting back tears.

"You may go, Lady Patricia, and right this instant." The dowager came to stand beside Sarah. "In all my life I have never known such a callous and cold person such as you. These are not the actions of a lady."

Lady Patricia lifted her nose and walked off. Sarah met her ladyship's gaze and smiled. "Thank you."

"You're very welcome, my dear." Her ladyship patted her hand. "May I have a word, Sarah?"

She nodded. "Of course."

"I do not know what has happened between you and my grandson today, and to be frank I do not wish to. But I do know my daughter in law has played a hand in this and, for that, I am sorry for you and Eric."

Sarah shook her head. "It was entirely my fault. This whole...everything that went wrong is because of me. Please do not blame him. Let it go and just be there for him when I leave—that is all I ask."

"But he loves you still, my dear. Is there no way to reconcile?"

"No, there is not." The words were as hollow as her heart.

"Can you not try, my dear?" The dowager squeezed her hand. "Can you not stay?"

Sarah met her gaze, and the desperate edge the other woman's voice brought tears to her eyes. She bit her lip and shook her head, unable to trust her voice.

"Very well. I suppose we will have to let you go."

Sarah nodded wishing that was not the case. "Yes, you do."

They both turned when Anita's father stopped the orchestra and caught the attention of the guests. With pride, he notified everyone that Anita and Lord Kentum would wed the following year.

The announcement of the new, but much longed for, betrothal of Lord Earnston and Lady Patricia followed. Mortified, Sarah raised her chin at the noticeable silence that ensued. Some guests glanced her way before everyone clapped for the happy couples.

It took all of Sarah's will not to flee. Eric was marrying Lady Patricia! It had barely been a few hours since he'd parted with her, and now he was betrothed to a woman Sarah knew he detested. How could he do something so hurtful to them both? And yet how could he not? She was not only the reason his brother was dead, but she'd used Eric, too, for her own means. Had it not been Lady Patricia, it would only have been someone else to whom he was betrothed, and rightfully so. She was not for him, and it was something she should have reminded herself of more often.

"I'm so sorry, Sarah." Her ladyship squeezed her hand again.

Sarah swallowed the lump in her throat. "So am I." A tear slid down her cheek, but she hastily brushed it away. In front of everyone, Eric placed a solitaire sapphire on Lady Patricia's finger and kissed it, then glanced out over the throng and found Sarah.

Telling herself she would not cry, she met his gaze and held it. With everyone else, she raised her glass in salute to the newly betrothed. Eric looked away first.

As soon as it was politely possible, she bid goodnight to Eric's grandmother and Anita, and left the ball. It was time to pack... Time to leave.

☙❦❧

SHE DIDN'T SLEEP THAT NIGHT. INSTEAD, SHE ORGANIZED her trunk, preparing for the journey back to the capital. She had written Eric a letter, explaining as much as she could in the hope it would ease his pain and anger...in time. She studied the photo of herself before the Tower Bridge—a bridge that didn't yet exist in 1818—and slipped it into the letter before sealing it with wax.

In the early morn, a light knock sounded on her door, and she turned to see Anita peep around the wooden threshold.

"Can I come in, dearest?"

"Of course." Sarah waved her in.

"So it is true? I heard from Eric at breakfast you're leaving today. Please say it isn't so?"

Sarah shrugged. "I'm afraid it is. You know I cannot stay. Especially since everyone else is departing after celebrating the betrothals being announced around here like wild fire."

She tried to smile at her half-hearted joke, but her friend's obvious sadness mimicked her own wretchedness. For the first time, Sarah lost her hold on her emotions. Warm, comforting arms wrapped around her and rubbed her back.

Before Sarah's tears were finished, a maid walked in and notified them the post chaise had arrived. While footmen collected her trunk, Anita walked her to the foyer.

"I will meet you outside."

Sarah followed her friend's steps before turning and facing the library door. She pulled the letter from her pocket and placed it on the silver salver near the entrance. Eric would read the letters later in the day, long after she was gone.

Walking toward the library, she knocked twice, waited for his reply and entered. Her steps faltered when she saw him. Gone was the gentleman who slept well and looked after his appearance, replaced by a man who appeared tormented and far from all right. His hair was askew, and he still sported the same clothes he'd worn to the ball the previous evening. She frowned.

"What do you want? I think we've said everything that needed to be said yesterday, wouldn't you agree?"

Sarah held her hands to keep them from trembling. "I just wanted to say that I am truly sorry for what happened between us, Eric. I never meant to hurt you or your family. I will forever regret the night your brother died. He was an honorable man who saved me, but to his own detriment." She paused. "I am also sorry for allowing us to form an attachment. It was wrong and, as much as I regret the hurt I've caused you, I cannot regret what we had."

She motioned out the window at the carriage that awaited her. "As you can see, we're about to go, and well, I just wanted to say that…What I needed you to know is…" She stopped and frowned. "You're a wonderful man, and you deserve to be happy. I want you to have a family, become a father. Promise me you will have a good life, or at least try to."

Outside, the driver called that all was ready for departure. Panic assailed her, knowing she had to go and that this was the last time she would ever see him.

Clutching her sickened stomach, she faced Eric, willing herself not to cry at the wretchedness she saw on his face. "I suppose this is goodbye then." She cleared her throat, needing to say what she must lest she regret it for the rest of her life. "I'll miss you. I want you to know that. I'll miss you my whole life." She turned to open the door and paused. Taking a deep breath, she met his gaze. "I love you," she said, then walked out the room and out of his life.

Forever.

ERIC COULD NEITHER MOVE NOR SPEAK. SHE LOVED HIM? Was she really leaving? Of course she was. He'd told her to get out himself. He swore. Walking to the window, he watched as her carriage pulled away, taking a piece of his heart with it. He turned away and strode to his desk, sick with grief, sick within himself at what he had hastily said to her yesterday. Hurt her as she'd hurt him.

And, dear God, the pain would surely tear him in two. What had he done? He silently castigated himself. He was now engaged to a woman he'd known all his life, but hardly knew well and cared even less about. He had insulted and belittled the woman he loved, cherished, and adored.

What he had said to her yesterday—he wasn't a gentleman, he was an arse.

It was absurd, making out he did not care for her—deluding one's self was never healthy. And knowing he had requested Lady Patricia's hand in marriage made his blood run cold. He would regret that vindictive decision for the rest of his life.

The dejection on Sarah's face when the announcements were made had cut him in two. It didn't help that his grandmother's disappointment only added to his injury.

He'd slept in the library last night, not trusting himself to even walk past Sarah's room. Knew he was likely to storm within and beg for forgiveness. Beg her not to leave him. Beg her to stay.

No matter what she'd said about feeling responsible for William's death. Logic told him he couldn't lay the fault entirely at her door. But archeologist? Time traveler? A woman who worked, earned money supposedly, and wasn't interested in marriage? Sarah had to have a maggot in her head over the fanciful lie she'd sported. He was a peer of his realm, a man with responsibilities and duties; he couldn't marry a woman touched in the upper works.

The memory of her teasing him over his portrait assailed him. Was he too serious and proud? Fury at his own stupid, ridiculous pride tormented him. He would never again feel her snuggled against him, laughing up at him with those gorgeous emerald green eyes and exquisite dimples beside her lips.

However, the thought of her stealing from his brother and partaking in his death, not to mention living with a man who wasn't a relative, soon pushed such thoughts aside. The devil nagged him, and his self-respect would not allow for total forgiveness.

It was for the best he gave Sarah the conge. Really, he should be relieved he'd escaped the clutches of such a wench.

Lifting the desk, he threw it, overturning the heavy piece of furniture, spilling its contents to the floor. Running a hand through his hair, he gripped his head in torment. Turning, he took in the side gardens, the colors blending through his vision. He was a fool.

A fool who let pride rule his head.

A fool who had lost the only thing in the world he had ever wanted.

Sarah.

CHAPTER 19

SARAH SLUMPED onto the suede lounge in her father's house and flicked on the TV. A re-run of *Oprah* discussing lost loves, of all things. She flicked the channel over to the news and stared unseeing at that instead.

It had been forty-five days since she'd left Eric, and she was keenly aware of every sixty-four-thousand-eight-hundred minutes as they ticked away. She flicked a switch on the electronic device beside the lounge and welcomed the dark as the blinds started to close. Shutting her eyes, she pictured Eric. In the quiet, she could almost feel and hear him again.

The lounge door opened, severing her memories.

"Sit up, Sarah." Her father walked in and sat down across from her. He stared at her for a moment, then sighed.

"What's the matter? Has something happened? Is everything okay at TimeArch?" Her father's silence was unnerving, and her hands trembled.

"Get dressed. I have to take you somewhere." He paused, his face strained. "We need to talk."

Taken aback, but hearing the urgency, she quickly did as he'd asked. On the way out the front door, she caught a glimpse of her reflection and stopped.

There were dark rings beneath her eyes, and her hair needed washing. She'd lost weight, too, her clothes hanging off her frame.

Disgust at her self-pity made her cringe. She shouldn't do this to herself or her family. Grabbing her bag, she walked out to the company vehicle in the drive and buckled herself into the passenger seat.

Her fragile composure started to fray as the roads heading south out of London became all too familiar. Towns she'd passed through in a horse and carriage zoomed past her window. In the one hundred and ninety-six years since she'd last seen them, the trades and store-fronts had changed, but it didn't matter. Her gut still tightened into a ball of homesick knots.

Why would her father be so cruel as to drive her to Westerham? Just as she suspected, the car turned and continued toward another even more familiar location. Why in God's name would her father be taking her to Eric's ancestral home? How was she to summon the courage to walk through those doors? Her smiling, charismatic, caring, wonderful man would not come out to greet her this day. Her tears fell unchecked until her father, silently acknowledging her grief, passed her his hankie. She didn't feel better for it.

The car pulled up before Eric's home, and Sarah's gaze moved over the house and land as she stepped from the vehicle. Not much had changed over the passing years except the house now sported a plaque noting its historical significance to the area.

A UK National Trust sign stated the home was now under their care and responsibility. Unease crept along her skin over not knowing what had happened to the family.

The trees were bigger, and the maze a lot higher than it had been. There were obviously different plants in the garden beds surrounding the home, but the building was much as she'd known it. Handsome and welcoming, just like its fifth earl. The sound of water pulled her attention to the lake, and her heart squeezed. The day she and Eric had spent there would be one memory she'd cherish forever.

Grief, as severe as she'd ever known, tore at her heart. She missed him.

What was she doing here without him? Wiping her eyes, she tried to gain some semblance of control. She really could not mourn like this forever, could she? Probably yes, she conceded. At this moment, she couldn't see any light at the end of the tunnel, and it was looking to be a bloody long tunnel.

She followed her father up the front steps, through the grand oak doors, and into the foyer. Everything was essentially the same as when she'd left it. The wallpaper was slightly aged, and the carpet a little the worse for wear, but otherwise, everything was frighteningly familiar.

This beloved house was so familiar and comforting. A small smile lifted her lips as she found her feet silently moving toward the library.

Ignoring her father's banter with the caretaker, she opened the doors. The library was unchanged. The chairs were in their same positions before the hearth, which dominated the center of the room. Eric's desk still stood in front of the windows. She walked up to it, running her hand over the leather top. She could imagine him sitting behind it, bestowing on her the lovable, mischievous grin she adored so much.

She frowned down at the golden quill—the very one she had used to write the letter she'd left for him. Next to it, the family seal lay dry, covered by a slight film of dust. She picked it up, needing to hold anything she knew Eric had used numerous times. It was all so confusing and painful.

And why was there no family living here? What had happened to Eric? She chastised herself for wallowing in self-pity instead of finding out what had become of him and his family. Her father entered the room.

"What the hell is going on? Why did you bring me here when you know how difficult these past weeks have been?" She put down her precious link to Eric and leaned against the desk for support. "Where is his family? Why is there no earl in residence? This place resembles a shrine—" She broke off abruptly, hearing her voice wobble, and clapped her hand over her mouth, knowing she was near hysterical. "Please tell me what has happened; I need to know."

Her father held up his hand to stop the questions. "I'm sorry, darling, for bringing you here. I thought it might be hard for you, but I needed to see for myself how the memories would affect you."

Sarah frowned, thoroughly confused.

"I have to apologize if I've been angry with you of late. Some very big changes occurred while you were away. I didn't want to do this, Sarah, and you must know it breaks my heart to see you like this."

"Couldn't you have told me this at the office or at home?" Tears blurred her vision, completely distorting her view of her father. She heard him come toward her before he took her in his arms, rubbing her back comfortingly.

"Hush now. I need to show you something. I've booked the estate today so we won't be interrupted. Come, sit down, and I'll explain."

They sat in the leather chairs facing the unlit hearth. It was the most bizarre thing Sarah had ever done. It was as if she could still smell Eric's scent within the room. She blew her nose while waiting for her father to begin.

"I've been angry because although I didn't know what exactly happened to you in 1818, I know the basic facts. I know how attached you and Lord Earnston became. And, if family letters I've read are any indication, he was on the verge of proposing. To be frank, I was extremely furious at your lack of restraint and unethical work practices while you were away. But," he sighed, "I understand what happens when you fall in love. And I cannot for the life of me criticize you for what I have always tried to instill in you."

When lightning strikes, you should always follow your heart, not your head.

She'd heard the words a thousand times.

"So I can't now, after twenty-four years, turn around and change my mind. No matter what the company rules are," he said, chuckling wryly. "Do you forgive me?"

What was to forgive? Reaching across, she took his hands. "Of course I do, always, you know that."

He squeezed hers in response. "Research has brought to light some very important circumstances for this family, which occurred not long after you left 1818. Some of these are new to history, thanks to your trip." He pointedly raised an eyebrow, which made Sarah wince. TimeArch employees weren't supposed to change history by interacting with it, and she'd done it not once but twice. "You need to know what occurred, no matter how painful." He sat back in his chair, his gaze never wavering.

Apprehension settled over Sarah. Her gut knotted spring-tight, and her hands started to sweat.

"Lord Earnston married a woman named Lady

Patricia Meyers not long after you left. Within two months of the marriage, both the new countess and his mother, Lady Earnston, were killed in a carriage accident just north of here."

Sarah gasped. Poor Eric, he had lost her, then two members of his immediate family. And she had not been there for him. She might never have been on good terms with either woman, but she wished death upon no one. Eric's mother would not have been fifty-five, she mused, and as for Lady Patricia, she was younger than Sarah herself was now.

"From paper records, family letters, and so on, I gather Eric lived fairly hard and fast for a couple of years after that. He never remarried, gambled heavily for a time, but finally pulled himself out of that, which was something, I suppose." She half-smiled at her father's distaste. She put Eric's choices down to grief.

"He wasn't seen much in society after 1819 and pretty much kept to himself. He passed away in his sleep in the autumn of 1878."

Sarah wiped her eyes, sniffing. "So Eric is buried here on the family estate?"

"Yes, he's buried here, and it's where we're going next. There's something you need to see." He looked across to her in concern. "Are you up to it, darling?"

Was she? "Of course," she said, though she wasn't at all as sure as she tried to sound. She felt slightly light-headed.

They made their way toward the family mausoleum on the northern hill behind the estate. It was a beautiful final resting place, overlooking the family's land.

The groundskeeper dislodged years of dust as he unlocked and opened the creaking steel doors. He lit the candles in the circular building, casting light on the family headstones that lined the walls.

Sarah started to read the epitaphs. Lady Patricia's grave identified her as the Countess of Earnston. Wiping her eyes, Sarah comprehended just how much time had passed. It was so final.

She found Eric's grandmother's grave, and her heart broke at the sight of it. The inscription read "left this world in the year of our Lord 1828," only ten short years after her departure.

"Come here, Sarah."

Pulling her thoughts back from the past, she turned and joined her father in front of a large, ornate sarcophagus. She knew whose it was before she reached it. Tears burned her eyes, blurring her vision.

Crouching, she ran her hand along Eric's name as she searched out the date of his death. She smiled; her father was never wrong: 1878. He'd been eighty-six years young. She stared at the cross carved above his name before reading the full inscription. She hadn't known his middle name was Sebastian.

She was happy he lived a long life, but it saddened her that, after losing Patricia, he'd avoided company or love. Ironically, she now faced the same fate. There would be no other man for her.

She stood, staring down at his grave, realizing what she had to do. The oppressive weight that had settled on her lifted with her decision, and she knew it was the right one.

She could not allow their lives to end like this. For her to live a full and happy life, to have any future at all, it would have to be in the past, with Eric.

"Sarah, will you read the inscription on the side? I understand Lord Earnston noted his desire to have it carved in his will."

Walking over, she knelt beside him. She squinted, struggling to read the script not fully illumined by the candles. Her hands shook as she deciphered the words.

The message read: *I believe. I love and miss you. Please come back to me. Eric.*

She sought her father's hand as her heart raced. She could almost hear his voice saying the words, and she shivered as a breeze caressed her skin. Her father's arms came around to embrace her.

Her heart shattered. Eric had waited so long for her— waited his whole life for a woman who never came back. She looked at her father, only to see he already knew what she was about to say.

"I know, my girl. I know what has to be done and, although it will probably kill me, seeing you like this is worse. You have to go back, build your life with him. I won't stand in your way."

Crying with relief, Sarah hugged him. She understood what a profound and heart-wrenching sacrifice he was making as a parent. "I don't know what to say. Thank you doesn't seem enough."

"Yes, I know. I also know there is no point in two people living miserable lives when it doesn't have to be that way. And that's why I'm sending you back. He obviously mourned you his whole life, and I refuse to allow you to do the same." He wiped at his eyes. "So if I have to let you go I will. I'll do it for you both."

"But, what about changing history? Won't my going back, staying, and creating a life with Eric possibly cause havoc in the future?"

"You are changing history, but for the better. No harm will come to this time other than the fact that this estate will hopefully be under the family's care and not the National Trust's. And that I may possibly have grandchildren, too." Her lips trembled as her father's voice broke with emotion. "I know you will have a wonderful life, full of love and happiness, and that is enough to make me never regret my decision. I love you, kiddo."

She gave him a fierce hug. "I love you, too. I'll miss you."

"Only mad scientists like me would get away with something like this." He laughed. "So it's lucky for you, my girl, that I'm one of those."

Sarah hugged him tighter. "You're not a mad scientist; you're a brilliant mad scientist."

Both laughed as Sarah re-read the carved message on Eric's grave. She silently promised him she would take heed of his final request and come home.

To him.

CHAPTER 20

It was another week before Sarah could depart. Her father needed the time to cover all legalities—and to ensure that if Eric would not take her back, or died having never married her, she would be protected and comfortable.

TimeArch staff traveled back and opened an account at Lloyds Bank with a deposit large enough to last two lifetimes. The Mayfair home they'd previously used was purchased, and the deeds were transferred into her name. By the close of the day, she returned to 1819, the house would be fully staffed by nineteenth century workers hired from an employment agency of the time.

At last, Sarah waited in her father's office, clicking a pen on and off as she counted down the time before she left.

"Ready to ride, Sarah?"

She looked up at her dad. "I am." She stood up and kissed him, threw her arms around him to hug him one last time. "I love you. I'll miss you, and take care of yourself, won't you?"

He smiled at her. "Of course I will. Don't you worry

about me. Just make me proud by marrying your earl and living a wonderful life. That will be enough for all of us at TimeArch." He paused. "But, Sarah, I do want to make sure you are certain. You know after being back in the past for a certain amount of time, you cannot return home. Time is fickle and waits for no one. I'd hate for you to regret your choice and come back here only to find yourself older than you ought to be."

Sarah nodded, knowing only too well how final this day would be. "You're referring to how time moves at different speeds when time traveling? I understand the risk, and I'm 100 percent sure."

He kissed her forehead. "Okay, then."

They made their way to the time machine, and apprehension rolled through Sarah's every pore. Would Eric take her back or would it take years of work on her part to earn his trust and love again—despite what he'd had engraved on his tomb? She steeled herself to win, no matter the cost. She loved him and knew he'd forgiven her at some point in his life. There had to be a way to reconcile, and she was damned well determined to find it.

Pulling on the brightest smile she could, she blew her father a good-bye kiss and waved. Then she silently said farewell to her twenty-first century life and welcomed back the nineteenth century with open arms.

THE STAFF BEGAN ARRIVING JUST AFTER LUNCH. SARAH WAS pleasantly surprised with their professionalism and wonderful manners. She was also glad none of them raised their eyebrows at their employer being a young, unmarried woman living alone without a companion.

During the first few days back in town, she kept to

herself, ordering new dresses and getting to know her staff. She sent her head groom to purchase a carriage and horses from Tattersalls, since it was frowned on for women to go there themselves.

Eric had not seen her for over a year—it was 1819, and the current Season was ending, families returning to their country estates to spend Christmas and New Year away from the city.

Perusing one of the period's gossip sheets, Sarah smiled when she read the wedding announcement for Anita and Lord Kentum. They were to be married next Saturday at Eric's country estate.

Scribbling a short missive, she sent a footman to deliver the letter notifying her friend of her return to London. Just as she sat down to a cup of tea an hour or so later, her parlor door burst open, and a whirlwind of color flew into the room and ran toward her.

Sarah jumped up, laughing, and held her arms out to Anita. They pulled apart, smiling through their tears, hands enfolded.

"Sarah, you can't imagine my joy on receiving your letter today. I nearly screamed the house down and immediately ordered the carriage to be brought round. Mother almost had a seizure."

Sarah laughed, imagining the scene her letter would have created. "I've missed you, too, my dear friend. I'm so glad you came." She pulled Anita down to sit beside her.

"How is it that you are here?"

Sarah smiled and shrugged, telling Anita the truth when she said, "I couldn't stay away. I belong in London and feel at home here. My future is here."

"Oh, Sarah." Anita paused. "So you plan on staying? For good?"

Sarah laughed. "Yes, I'm staying for good. Now tell me

all the gossip. I understand you're to be married next week-end." She grinned. "Poor old Lord Kentum, still waiting to see that silk shift? How he must be suffering, poor man."

Anita laughed lovingly, her eyes bright with joy. "I see you still read that gossip page. And yes, Freddie and I will at long last be married on Saturday." She wearily sighed. "It's been very trying these last months, not being able to marry. But with Lord Earnston's mother and wife dying…" She hesitated until Sarah nodded for her to continue. "Well, the whole family went into mourning, which put the marriage off for several months. It's been very hard, and Eric…"

Sarah's gaze flew to her friend. "What's wrong with Eric? Has something happened to him?" *Please God, no*, she silently begged.

"No, no nothing like that, he's fine in that sense. However, he is no longer the Eric you and I once knew. Since you left, he's been very different. His marriage— well, that didn't help because, let's face it, it was a disaster. And we have not been able to pull him out of whatever hole he has himself buried in." Anita sighed. "The whole family is worried. He gambles heavily, hardly associates with any of us, and no longer spends any time with his friends."

Shocked, Sarah simply stared at Anita. Her father had told her what he knew of Eric's life after her 1818 disappearance; nevertheless, it hurt her to learn the extent of his dissolute existence.

"Do you think Eric would be willing to see me? I know we didn't part on good terms, but he was a good friend once." Inwardly, she cringed at using the word *friend*. She'd been far from just a friend to the man. "Maybe I would be able to help."

Anita grabbed her hand, squeezing it. "You know Eric

would see you in a flash. Don't think to hide what I know you felt for each other. You were in love with him, and still are. And it's plain to all, Eric is still in love with you."

Sarah's heart flipped at hearing that spoken aloud. "Why, whenever I mention your name he storms from the room, and it's been over a year since my betrothal party." Anita grinned, the devil entering her eye. "Oh yes, my friend, my darling cousin most certainly still loves you, and I will ensure that you, Miss Baxter, marry that man if it's the last thing I do on this planet."

Sarah laughed, agreeing wholeheartedly with her idea. "Well then, we'd better come up with a plan, what do you say?"

"Absolutely," Anita replied, her smile triumphant.

ANITA'S WEDDING WAS UNPRETENTIOUS BUT ELEGANT—THE small chapel on Eric's estate filled with friends and family. An ethereal quality radiated from the bride, and Lord Kentum beamed like a man truly besotted as he watched Anita glide toward him. Sarah's eyes misted as they said their vows. She smiled across at Eric's grandmother, who appeared extremely happy at her appearance at the wedding. It was so moving to witness a couple who meant every word of their marriage vows.

The wedding ceremony was shorter than Sarah had expected, and she wondered why they had not kissed when declared man and wife. But then the poor couple had waited so long to marry, perhaps it was no wonder the ceremony seemed hasty.

Sarah threw white rose petals at the happy bride and groom as they walked from the chapel. Standing back, she studied the guests, vastly disappointed that Eric had chosen not to come.

Anita's family was hosting a wedding breakfast at Eric's estate before the bride and groom left for their honeymoon on the continent. The newly married pair left in Lord Kentum's carriage, while Sarah's heart yearned for a similar situation between her and Eric.

Sometime later, she stood under a marquee, the smell of flowers and the sound of laugher floating in the air. She skimmed the surrounding crowd of family and friends, willing the one man she wanted to see to appear.

How could he not be here! Having given up hope of seeing Eric, she took a bite of cake and decided to at least enjoy the delicious fare on offer. A tittering of conversation went through some of the guests standing nearby, and her skin prickled with awareness. Her attention was pulled across the lawn, and there he stood.

She sucked in a startled breath at the vision he made. Stylishly dressed despite the absence of a cravat, he was thinner than she remembered, his hair messier, almost bedraggled, in fact. He was no doubt inebriated.

Sarah swallowed the stab of jealousy, wondering what he'd been up to before coming to express his congratulations to his cousin and her new husband. Still, she found herself unable to tear her eyes from him—even in disarray, he was more devastatingly handsome than she remembered. Her soul sang, and for the first time in months, she felt alive.

Then a very real worry settled in her belly. His eyes had a desolate blankness to them. She knew the look well, having seen it in the mirror merely two weeks ago. She frowned, seeing him standing against the terrace railing, not focusing on anything at all.

She watched to see if anyone would engage with him in conversation. People nodded as they passed, but no one stopped to chat. It seemed everyone, including his family, kept their distance from him these days.

It broke her heart when he threw down his glass of whisky in one gulp and immediately requested another from a passing footman.

Though she knew she was being a coward, hiding in the marquee behind a gaggle of matrons, she couldn't cross the lawn to let him know she was there. Still, she could not stand there like a mutant all day.

Sarah took a calming breath and stepped away from her hidey-hole to approach Lord and Lady Kentum, ostensibly to congratulate them once more. Anita held out her hand as she came toward them before leaning down to whisper in her ear.

"He is here, Sarah; have you seen him?" Anita scanned the garden in search of her cousin.

Sarah stood next to her, laughing at her matchmaking antics, and on her wedding day no less. "Yes, and it's a little troubling to see him like that. I'm starting to doubt he will speak to me; he's doesn't seem the most sociable at the moment."

Anita squeezed her hand in assurance. "He will, dearest. I know he will."

Other guests wanting to wish the couple happy bombarded the newly married pair. Sarah spent the whole time shaking in trepidation, wondering when Eric would notice her. She smiled as Eric's grandmother walked toward her and kissed her cheek.

"Sarah, my dear, I thought I would never see you again. Oh, my sweet girl, come give me a hug. I wanted to catch you in the church, but I lost sight of you before I could." Sarah leaned down and hugged the small but strong woman she had grown to love.

"You have no idea how happy you've made me, seeing you back in London, and at Anita's wedding breakfast, no less."

"I'm happy to be here as well, my lady. I hope you've been well." The dowager countess looked around the gardens. It wasn't hard to know who she was seeking out.

"I have kept myself reasonably busy since you went away. It has been a trying year and half, my dear—one I will be glad to forget. But you're here now, and Anita is now married—perhaps our family's fortune is turning."

Sarah smiled down at her ladyship, hoping the same. "I'm sure it is, my lady." She paused in thought. "I'm sorry to hear about Lady Earnston and Lady Patricia. I was saddened to hear of the accident."

Her ladyship sighed. "It's a sad tale, my dear—one I'm not going to go into today of all days," she replied while patting her hand. "Now, make sure you enjoy yourself. This wedding has been a long time coming."

Sarah could not agree more. "I can assure you, my lady, I will. Perhaps I could call on you tomorrow?"

"I would like that, dear. Now if you'll excuse me, I had better go make my address to the new Marchioness of Kentum."

Sarah laughed as the dowager walked away and made a beeline through the guests to Anita's side. She joined a group of unmarried girls who were conversing beside her and soon lost herself within the flow of conversation, as she waited patiently for fate to show its hand.

WHAT IN HELL WAS HE DOING HERE? ERIC HAD NO IDEA. He gazed scathingly at the throng of guests. His head pounded, and he needed sleep, not to mention a bath. Still, alcohol and idleness were a pleasant way to pass the time when there was nothing to live for.

He sighed, glancing over to his cousin who glowed with happiness. To see her so was why he'd come. He loved Anita like a sister and wanted to share her day. Well, what was left of it.

But the notion of being surrounded by happy couples, smiling, laughing, enjoying themselves, was enough to make him bristle with rancor.

His eyes narrowed as his temper flared. What he really wanted to do was throw something. Punch the lucky bastards who dared to be married and happy. Or better, seduce their women, ruining their marriages in the process, just so they could all be as miserable as he was.

He tried to sip his drink in a more gentlemanly fashion. He had to be losing it. Of late, he had been finding it harder and harder to keep himself together.

Eric took another sip of his drink. He wanted to die, no longer wanted to live with the agonizing pain of her absence. An absence that wore on his soul and left it empty.

He swirled the amber liquid in his glass. He couldn't do it. And all because he lived with the hope he'd see her again. Unlikely as that now seemed after so long. He would live out this hollow life, and alone, since Sarah was not ever coming back.

He drank the rest of his brandy, swaying as it hit his nearly empty stomach. A year and a half had passed since she left. There was no longer any hope of seeing her again. His soul severed in two, and he shut his eyes as he tried to push away the pain of such musings. He wanted her back.

He felt his chest, reassuring himself it was still there. Felt the square like paper beneath the fold of his suit and relaxed.

The picture of Sarah was never away from his person. So lifelike that it virtually enabled him to visualize touching her, to hear her again. His only link to her was starting to disintegrate from so much handling, and he was silently terrified of losing it.

His mind wandered back to that day. The missives placed upon his desk after lunch bore nothing of interest until his eyes alighted upon a letter in small, neat, flowing script. He cursed his weakness as his heart jumped when he recognized the sender. He opened it, not really knowing what to expect from her words. Read it repeatedly, devoured and memorized every word she wrote. It was days before he really studied the picture, he was so lost in his grief.

The vehicles in the picture's background were unknown to him. They were smooth and glossy, large and small, all in a magnitude of colors. The bridge he knew nothing of stood strong and proud across the Thames, beside the Tower of London. Her clothes and the people around her were also different. It dawned on him immediately that what she said was true—she was not of his time.

So, she wouldn't be in London next season. Christ, she wouldn't be of this realm. And in that moment, his hopes of seeing her again during his lifetime were lost. All that had been holding him together, all that he'd hoped for was gone. He had nothing.

He nodded to an acquaintance, his mind still on Sarah. He had been such a bastard, wanted nothing but to hurt her. Yes, she had been involved with William's death, but he could not blame her entirely. William always played the hero, and as much as he loved his brother, it wasn't Sarah's fault they fell.

Eric grabbed another glass of brandy from a passing footman. He shot the drink down, eyes watering from the burning sensation it caused. He had been walking dead for months, day after day of endless emptiness.

It was enough to push any man to his limits, and he was certainly at the edge. He knew he would have to curtail his downward spiral before he lost it all. But how the hell was he to do that, without *her*?

Keeping to the edge of the gathered throng, he realized another meaningless day had passed him by. He should be sociable with his family and acquaintances here, but the ability to be civil was now an absent characteristic in his body's composition.

He rubbed his jaw and sighed. He would have to give his felicitations to the happy couple, but that would be the limit of his speech. He had grown fond of the fact that no one spoke to him anymore. He did not want their small-minded, boring chitchat in his ears in any case. All he longed for was to hear one voice above all speak to him, just once more.

"Hello, Eric."

His brandy glass fell unheeded, splashing amber liquid over his boots. Heart in his mouth, he forgot to breathe, seeing the vision before him. The world's axis tilted and he swore...loudly.

It was not possible!

Eric swallowed the lump in his throat as he tried unsuccessfully to steady his shaking hands. Either he had drank more than he thought, or he was now so sick with grief that he was imagining Sarah. He rubbed a hand over his face, thinking to clear his vision. It did not.

The beautiful apparition in ivory silk was still beside him, smiling up at him...*enjoying herself*.

His jaw clenched.

His grandmother's comforting hand wrapped about his arm. "Eric, my dear. Say hello to Miss Baxter. She's returned to London."

Unable to comprehend his grandmother's words, he kept his eyes fixed on Sarah, not willing to look away in fear she would disappear into thin air like a tormenting ghost.

"Eric, are you well? You look like you've seen a ghost."

Eric's mouth lifted into a slight grin at his grandmother's declaration. Out of his peripheral vision, he could see Sarah's answering smirk. "An angel more like."

His grandmother nodded. "Is she not beautiful? Why don't you take Miss Baxter for a walk and ask her to marry you, and make sure, Eric dear, that she says yes this time. I do so adore family weddings."

Eric stilled at his grandmother's forward suggestion. The matriarch of his family strode away, and he marveled at her gumption.

Sarah stepped before him, and heat coursed through his blood. "Hello, Miss Baxter."

A FLUTTER OF AWARENESS PASSED OVER HER AS SHE HEARD the deep tenor of his voice. What an idiot she'd been to think she could live without this man. Silent emotions clashed between them; love, desire, anger, and sorrow all slammed into her with his look.

What would he do? What would he say? Not entirely sure his reaction to her return would be good, she lifted her chin and met his gaze. Around her, conversations ceased, and it seemed everyone present was waiting to see just what would transpire at their reunion.

"You took your pretty time coming back."

Sarah lost herself in the blue depths of his eyes and saw the unconditional love blazing from them and only for her. His hands came up to caress her cheeks, soft and worshipful, before sliding through her hair, scattering her pins to the floor. She placed her own hand atop his, realizing they were shaking.

"I'm sorry."

Eric shook his head in awe. "I'm the one who's sorry. God, I've missed you." He took her mouth in a searing kiss, declaring his claim to all who were present. Sarah ignored the startled gasps from guests, including the claps that came from the few Sarah assumed to be Anita and Lord Kentum.

Sarah inwardly laughed as Eric refused to release her. Not that she minded, as with every caress her soul came back to life. She would let him kiss her all day long if he wanted. She clasped his nape, standing on her toes to enable Eric to deepen the embrace. He was kissing her like a man starved of his life force. Tears burned behind her lids, and she let them fall unheeded.

Eric broke the kiss as a discreet cough brought them out of their sensual haze. He grinned, his love clear in his eyes. His tightly leashed resolve crumbled, and he hugged her to him, pulled her as close as possible before the laugh she loved as much as life itself sounded beside her ear.

"I can't believe it," he said, rocking her within his arms. "Is it really you? Oh my darling, I didn't think I would ever see you again." He frowned as he wiped tears from her cheeks.

"I've missed you, too. I love you. I'm sorry about our fight, about—" Eric kissed her, stemming her apology.

"Don't mention that awful day. I'm the one who should apologize. I believe what you told me about where you were from. You know that, don't you?"

Sarah nodded.

"I was a vile cad calling you those filthy names. I never meant a word of it. Please say you forgive me, my love."

Sarah threw her arms around him and snuggled into his chest. "Always. I could never stay angry at you for long, as you well know."

Eric laughed, the sound carefree and happy. He pulled back and caught her gaze, and Sarah let herself become lost in the blue depths of his eyes. "Marry me?"

Sarah smiled, allowing him to see how happy the question made her. She ran her fingers over his cheeks, the day's long stubble prickling her palms, before clasping his dark locks in her hands.

"Yes, I'll marry you, my lord."

"I don't deserve you, my love," he said, kissing her once more.

"Oh, yes you do." Sarah squeaked as Eric picked her up, both laughing like children, as he rained kisses on her face. Eventually, Eric set her down and turned to the enthralled crowd.

"Let it be known this day that Miss Sarah Baxter has done me the greatest honor of accepting my hand in marriage."

The guests, though all shocked, could not deny the love between the couple. With this much juicy gossip for tomorrow's social rounds, all heartily applauded the happy announcement. Eric sobered as his attention returned to her.

"You are all invited here next Saturday for our wedding." Sarah laughed as more cheers and congratulations sounded, before Eric led her toward the house. Sarah hastened her steps to keep up with his pace.

They entered a vacant parlor before continuing down a long corridor. Double glass doors signaled another room, and Eric bowed as he ushered her into the conservatory. She smiled when he dragged her to a cushioned iron sofa, pulling her onto his lap. The air was hot and heady with exotic perfumed plants. Water tinkled from a fountain, hidden behind the abundance of plants.

Unable to resist, she pulled him into a kiss. He had been gazing at her so adoringly, if she didn't do something, she would start crying again. How had she survived without him? She pulled away, needing to explain before they started their life together.

"Eric, I meant what I said. I am sorry for what I've put you through all these months. I want you to know I'm staying and I damn well will marry you, so you'd better have meant what you asked me outside."

Eric held her close. "You know I did. I missed you." He was silent for a moment as he regarded her. "I have to confess, it hasn't been a good time." Eric cleared his throat. "You've obviously heard what happened to my mother and Lady Patricia."

"I know everything that has happened in your life to date, Eric. There is nothing you have done that I do not know about. And even knowing all this does not make me love you less."

"I felt the biggest bastard after you left. I went through with the marriage because I had no other choice. I wanted to break the understanding, but Patricia would not hear of it. The whole situation was a mess."

Sarah kissed him, reassuring him as best she could. "I know."

"She deserved better than me, a man who not only

didn't love her but pined for another. My mother confessed her hatred toward you prior to the day of our falling out, and the rage I felt knowing you were their constant nemesis maddened me beyond belief. I couldn't forgive them."

He ran his hand through his hair. "Hell, I couldn't forgive myself, for that matter. I demanded they leave. I practically tossed them out the door. And of course you know what happened to their carriage as they returned to London."

Sarah kept silent, waiting for him to finish, knowing he needed to.

"I've spent the last months living in a hellish manner, and I'm not proud of it. I didn't believe your story, and I lost you, and I killed my mother and wife. I don't deserve to be happy."

Sarah refused to let him speak in such a way. "You do, Eric; don't ever say that. Why would you believe in time travel? The whole notion is quite absurd." She smiled. "And as for your mother and Lady Patricia, you weren't to know what would happen, just like the rest of us. It was an accident. You told me yourself the roads in this part of Kent could be perilous. I will not allow you to blame yourself, not now or ever.

"We have all acted irrationally out of fear, anger, love, and hate. We have all been fools, but we can't allow it to impinge on our future together. Let the past rest, my darling. Please do it for me. I don't care how you've lived since I left. I know you love me as I love you, and, as of today, we will begin anew. Agreed?" Smiling, she hugged him and kissed his cheek.

"I don't deserve to have you, Sarah. I cannot wait to make you my wife. I love you."

Sarah bombarded him with small kisses over his face,

desire heating her blood as his laugh rumbled within his tightly muscled chest.

"Yes you do, my lord. And I love you. So," Sarah said, pausing to undo his top shirt button, "let me prove it to you."

Eric growled, agreeing wholeheartedly as his hands ventured down her waist. "You already have proved it. You came back."

Dear Reader,

Thank you for taking the time to read *A Stolen Season*! I hope you enjoyed my Regency time travel romance. A Stolen Season was the first novel I ever wrote and combined my two great loves, time travel, and the Regency period. I hope you enjoyed Sarah and Eric's grand love that even time couldn't end.

I'm forever grateful to my readers, and I can't thank you enough for picking up and reading my books. If you're able, I would appreciate an honest review of *A Stolen Season*. As they say, feed an author, leave a <u>review</u>!

If you'd like to learn about my other time travel romances, may I suggest you start with my medieval time travel, Defiant Surrender? I have included the prologue for your reading pleasure.

Tamara Gill

DEFIANT SURRENDER

A love strong enough to withstand nine-hundred years…

Unlucky in love, Maddie St. Clair hides behind an antique store and her mudlarking hobby. That is until she finds a medieval ring that throws her back to 1102 Cumberland and into the life of Lady Madeline Vincent, heiress to Norman lands and about to be married to an autocratic Baron, William Dowell, nine hundred years her senior.

Lord William Dowell protects his own. Usually, from his closest neighbor and long standing foe the Baron of Aimecourt. Forced to marry his dead enemy's daughter, Lady Madeline, by King's decree, he hides his growing respect for his wife behind a wanton mistress. Yet when Madeline's life is threatened, William's loyalty to his kin is tested by the astonishing desire that flares between them. Not to mention the love that Madeline ignites that would last an eternity. If fate will allow . . .

PROLOGUE

England 1078 - Cumberland

VANESSA CUDDLED HER BABE CLOSE, the little girl's cry torn away by the raging wind. The air bit into her skin to the point of pain. Still, she waited. Would not leave until her lover's warming strength enclosed them both and gave them sanctuary.

She struggled to her feet as a door hidden within the stone walls of the gatehouse opened. A door she'd used often. The person she waited for and longed to see stepped forward. Wrapped in a fur cloak, he looked warm and well fed. His attractive visage with the short beard along his jaw heated her blood and inspired the desire to run her hands against his hard flesh.

"Why did you summon me, Vanessa?"

She started at the harshness of his words and looked into unforgiving eyes that were nothing like she remembered. His voice resonated with loathing and distaste, a tone he had never used before with her. Such severity was normally directed toward his wife or serfs. Never her.

"My lord, I have birthed our daughter. Look." She pulled the shawl away and smiled at the babe as love blossomed within her. "She is yours."

He cast their child a cursory glance before his eyes, vacant of warmth or interest, met hers again.

"What of it?"

"I had thought—" Vanessa's words trailed off. Her lover had become a stranger. She willed him to look at her as he once did, like a man in love who cared for her well-being and happiness. After all the months she had spent in his bed, had acquiesced to his every need it was not possible he could now feel...nothing! Panic tore through her breast when she realized the truth.

Vanessa pulled forth all the dignity she could muster, before lifting her chin as scornful eyes scrutinized her dirty gown and unwashed hair.

"What of it?" he asked again.

The cold penetrated Vanessa's thin shawl, but it was not the elements this night that made her shiver. His lordship's voice, emotionless and hard, chilled her blood and all hope dissipated.

"You had said, my lord—"

"What, woman?" he bellowed. "That I would take care of you?" His Lordship sneered. "Why, that babe is probably not even mine."

Vanessa gasped.

"You are a fool if you think I'll acknowledge your child as my blood. I have a wife, and a legitimate babe on the way to secure my wealth and family line. I've no need for a bastard. Off with you, woman! Do not let your shadow darken my lands again."

Dread crashed over her like a fallen tree. Vanessa's arms tightened with fear and the baby mewed in protest. She eased her hold and stepped forward.

"But, my lord, where will we go? I have nothing. My family are not even from these parts." She grabbed at his arm, stumbling when he wrenched it away. "Anthony," she pleaded, "you must help me!" Tears welled at such harsh treatment. Vanessa shook her head. Her heart refused to acknowledge his callous, cold manner, though her mind reeled. He no longer loved her, nor even cared.

She had been used as a temporary bedmate for a peer of the realm.

His hawk-like features revealed no trace of sympathy as he reached into his pocket, pulling out some coins, and throwing them at her feet. The hem of his fur cloak slapped her leg as he turned and ordered the door bolted. The sound of the lock putting paid to her services.

Vanessa bent down, picked up the minuscule amount of coin and stared, stunned, at the cold stone structure. With the wooden door now firmly shut in her face, there was little choice but to place the meager amount into her pocket. She swallowed threatening tears as the taunting sound of the guard's laughter echoed behind the oak. Distant flickering lights paved her way toward the village and she wrapped the shawl tighter around them both and walked away.

She needed to get back to London. Could only pray her family would welcome her, with a bastard child in tow.

She turned and looked back toward Aimecourt Castle. Anger coursed through her like a burning flame, evaporating any love she once felt for his lordship.

No man treated Vanessa Boulogne in such a way. The Baron of Aimecourt would be the first and last man, she silently vowed, to treat her like a piece of meat to be tossed to the wolves once his own gut was gorged and his hunger quelled.

No, Anthony Vincent would rue the day he had used

her so. Chin high and back steely straight, Vanessa walked into the night shadows and an unknown future, promising revenge.

Aimecourt and its grand baron would pay.

LORDS OF LONDON - BOOKS 4-6 BUNDLE

To Marry a Rogue Series
ONLY AN EARL WILL DO
ONLY A DUKE WILL DO
ONLY A VISCOUNT WILL DO

A Time Traveler's Highland Love Series
TO CONQUER A SCOT
TO SAVE A SAVAGE SCOT

Time Travel Romance
DEFIANT SURRENDER
A STOLEN SEASON

Scandalous London Series
A GENTLEMAN'S PROMISE
A CAPTAIN'S ORDER
A MARRIAGE MADE IN MAYFAIR
SCANDALOUS LONDON - BOOKS 1-3 BUNDLE

High Seas & High Stakes Series
HIS LADY SMUGGLER
HER GENTLEMAN PIRATE
HIGH SEAS & HIGH STAKES - BOOKS 1-2 BUNDLE

Daughters Of The Gods Series
BANISHED-GUARDIAN-FALLEN
DAUGHTERS OF THE GODS - BOOKS 1-3 BUNDLE

ABOUT THE AUTHOR

Tamara is an Australian author who grew up in an old mining town in country South Australia, where her love of history was founded. So much so, she made her darling husband travel to the UK for their honeymoon, where she dragged him from one historical monument and castle to another.

A mother of three, her two little gentlemen in the making, a future lady (she hopes) and a part-time job keep her busy in the real world, but whenever she gets a moment's peace she loves to write romance novels in an array of genres, including regency, medieval and time travel.

www.tamaragill.com
tamaragillauthor@gmail.com

CPSIA information can be obtained
at www.ICGtesting.com
Printed in the USA
BVHW041430170720
583973BV00010B/544